Velvet Spring

VELVET SPRING

Dede Reed

ISBN 978-1-97776-340-2

Book design: Lauren Harms
Cover art: Alexander Deineka, Portrait of a Girl with a Book, 1934.
©2017, State Russian Museum, St Petersburg.

Special thanks to Christine Schutt, Mike Levine, Elizabeth Yarborough, Bo Niles, Tamara Lloyd, Ene Riisna, Janny Goss, Lenny Golay, Peggy Watson, Bill Dewey, Jane Dewey, Nancy Greenway, and Colin Ferenbach.

Printed in the United States of America.

Plaindealing Press
P.O. Box 156
Royal Oak, Maryland

For Ene and Tamara

"For the mind, everything is in the future,
for the heart, everything is in the past."

ANDREI PLATONOV

ZOFIE

Pavlas House
Bohemia

In a hurry, Uršula had left me on the hearth while she ran to collect laundry whipping in the wind. The log crackled and broke apart. A spark fell on the blanket fringe. The linen, I was told, was beginning to smoke when Uršula ran back into the kitchen, picked me up, took me to the sink, and doused me with water. As she unwound the damp blanket that first morning, she noticed the name "Zofie" embroidered in the hem.

Uršula, forty years old, was unnerved from caring for an infant—a five-month-old abandoned child—who had been left outside her house on August 22, 1968. Years later, Uršula, in a rare moment of openness, told me how a hunched form, carrying something in his arms, had scurried from the shed to the chicken hutch and then to the front door. Gusts of wind were blowing in from the fields, shaking the limbs of the fruit trees, a shutter banged, and the sky was darkening. There was my cry. She opened the door to a baby. A baby she did not wish for, a baby that roused in her anxiety and confusion and fear, a baby she would have to make room for, to hold, to feed, to worry about.

"I heard that some people fled the country the day after the Russian invasion," she said—still says—when I ask who I might be, where I came from, who my parents were, why I had been left.

Measurements from her childhood—dates and ages—ascended the doorway. A carved line when Uršula was three. A red line indicated her heights at five and seven. Blue lines had been scratched in the doorway for her brother, Milan, when he'd been seven and nine and twelve. There were lines for her father with the dates 1910, 1914.

"Your hair. It's thick, has color. Mine is mousy." Uršula told me to stand in the pantry doorway, to lean back. She took a pencil from the shelf, pushed me against the molding, placed the pencil over my head, and scratched a lead line into the paint. "Now you are part of the Pavlas family. You at six are already taller than I was at eight."

Uršula marched in the morning to the chicken house, carried overflowing baskets of laundry from the sink to the clothesline, mopped the bathroom and kitchen floors with rags. She made breakfast for men who boarded at her house. Her eyes disappeared into slits when she spoke. She muttered as she wound wool. She stood over the vat of boiling jars as they clanked. Her knife sawed back and forth through fat and leftover meat. Her sausage-shaped fingers mixed the meat with shredded cabbage and put it in clay pots that were stored in the icebox. She baked biscuits, cherry puddings, roast pork, stewed mutton. She shook her finger when I washed dishes and did not save gristle to be minced and used in terrines. On Mondays she prepared porcelain jars of farmers cheese she cured in the cool of the pantry. She heated an iron on the wood stove to iron our blouses. She ironed sheets, pressing hard, with steam rising from the damp cotton, the board creaking from her weight. On Saturdays, she gave me an ironed apron.

"Do not get it dirty. It's to last all week."

I stood on a chair and stirred wheat germ and wholewheat flour, fanning the powder to keep it away from my face. I dug my fingers into warm yeast and rye, then shaped the dough to knead it. I cleaned seeds out of peppers, stuffed them with rice and carrots and minced meat. I peeled the skin from apricots or plums or apples and sliced mushrooms to dry on the windowsill. Plum juice squirted. Dirt from mushrooms got on my apron. Nedda, with wet paws, jumped on my lap. A bucket of mopping water I was dumping in the yard splashed.

Fridays, I cleaned the chicken coop. In other chores I raked leaves, spread burlap over the roses, harvested the last of the beets and parsnips. I collected fruit. Nedda followed me, meowing, her tail rubbing my leg as I filled the watering can or swept the steps. Summers in Bohemia were hot. Orange nasturtiums spilled from window boxes. The daisies in Uršula's garden drooped midday. By the end of the summer there was always a water shortage, and Uršula told me not to water the garden from the house well. Evenings, I carried buckets to the stream, sat down on the bank, kicked off my wooden sandals, and dipped my feet for a few moments.

On Saturdays Uršula and I walked down our road through a swale to the train station for the half-hour journey to Mesto Touskov to visit her only old friend. She liked to collect blackberries or wildflowers along the roadside. We crossed Rozm Brook, where I stopped to throw pebbles and listened for the pleasing plinking sound. Ahead was Uršula, her hips filling her nylon blue-flowered dress, her feet stuffed into two-inch high heels, a satchel digging into her shoulder and holding dumplings, bread, and sausages she had made for her friend. I ran to catch up, wearing my plaid pleated skirt, scuffed shoes, and a straw hat. Uršula never waited, and when I caught up, she always said, "Come along, come along." I was panting, imagining she'd disappear before I could reach for her hand, which she never gave to me.

The train crept up the hill through fields, past the ruins of Sitkova, past stone walls before the tracks curved along the Rybnik Svet Pond. There were the red-tiled roofs of town, the tree-lined Brezanova Street that wound to the Augustinian monastery. I sat in the foyer of Uršula's friend's apartment. Uršula's friend did not like children, would not let me come in, so I peered out the front door and noticed children from an orphanage. Their left hands were tied into loops of rope to keep them in line. The children were frisky, kicking each other, poking the person in front. The boys' hair was shaved, the girls' hair was under gray kerchiefs. They laughed; their cheeks were pink, their eyes mischievous.

I watched a mother and her two daughters come out of a clothing store. One girl skipped up the street, the other hugged a package, the mother stopped to light a cigarette. A man sitting on a bench threw breadcrumbs on the sidewalk. Pigeons flew from windowsills and trees, landing at the man's feet.

I heard steps creaking, thought it might be the woman who cleaned the building, who would often stare at me standing at the door, but it was Uršula, ready to continue our errands. She had her list: yeast and gelatin at the grocery, soap and dishtowels at a stand in the outdoor market, and sausage casings and lard at the butcher shop. Once a month, we'd stop to buy jar lids for Uršula's canning. "Pocket money," she'd say, patting her purse, thinking, perhaps, about the jams she'd sell. She steered me through narrow streets where gypsies lived in camps in tin lean-tos or round-roofed trailers.

"This is where children have been left. Look at the water closets perched over the gutters. Look at that pipe. Children here don't go to school. This is where they learn to steal."

A pipe stuck out from a cement wall. A dark-skinned woman rubbed clothes in a shallow pan, rinsed frayed, gray underpants under spurts of water, then beat out the moisture. A slapping echoed until we left the alley to walk to the tram to get to the train.

In 1979, when I was eleven, the Communist Party classified Uršula's house as an official government hostel for engineers and educational supervisors. One evening, during a power outage, Uršula and I were sitting in the kitchen, eating supper under the kerosene lamp. A car drove up to the house. The sound of the motor ripped open the silence. It chugged, clanked to a stop. Headlights beamed, illuminating the fog with rays of light, glaring as if from the armament factory yard. Two men got out. One was big, the other skinny and tall. They grabbed cardboard suitcases from the back seat, turned off the headlights, and slammed the doors.

I stood up from the table.

"Wait," Uršula said, holding her arm out to stop me. "I am not a servant."

After a few moments, Uršula got up, picked up the lantern, and went to open the door.

The men stepped into the hall and looked around. The big one said, "I am Comrade Jakub Milschek. My partner is Comrade Franta Petrovic." He waved an official piece of paper in Uršula's face. "We have orders to stay here for five months. Breakfast at seven. Dinner at nineteen hours." He leaned down and picked up his suitcase. They wore baggy suits, pointed shoes, fedora hats. One had a potbelly, the other had a long chin. They smelled like cigarettes.

Uršula led them, the lantern in her hand. She teetered as she walked, her face hard. Her dress swayed as she went up the dark stairwell. Light bounced from wall to wall. After the death of her parents, Uršula had been left to make her way as a caretaker of the boarding house. She scrubbed sweat from the boarders' shirts, cleaned stains in the toilet, ironed pants, split kindling, kneaded dough, and made jam that they ate by the spoonful. Along came rude men, an odd retired ornithologist, me, East Germans, and now men from Prague.

A few weeks after the government apparatchiks arrived at our house, I was transferred from the rural Leninski Skolni in the village and moved into Neculai Skolni, a thirty-minute train ride away, in Plzen. From the moment I walked into the school, and for months after, the girls in the class glared at me. I was new, wearing my own clothes—my school uniform had not arrived. The girls were a year older. For some reason I had been tested at Leninski and then placed in the higher-level gymnasium program, where I would not only continue German, but also begin to learn Russian.

One girl, the tallest, pulled at the lumpy sleeve of my sweater. "Did you knit this? It looks homemade." Her friends laughed. During lunch that first day, they turned their backs and walked off, whispering. In geography class, I raised my hand to answer a question about the capitals of the countries that bordered the Black Sea. After I said, "Bucharest, Sofia, Kiev, Moscow, Ankara, Tbilisi," I heard sighs of disgust and knew I would never fit in.

"Tell me," Uršula said, the first night after school when I would not answer her questions. "The gymnasium is not good?" But I knew by her frown and her voice that she was asking me what was wrong. She stared and stared at my report cards from Neculai, and tacked them along a shelf in the sitting room. "This is good," she'd say. I had by then more schooling than she.

I retreated to my room when the boarders came home. Uršula stayed in the pantry while they ate, awaiting demands for more stuffed cabbage, dumplings, beer. The men lingered, slurping soup, belching, laughing, arguing about agricultural collectives, about industrialization.

"Wait," Uršula said to me one morning as I was walking out the door to go to school. "I am going to come." When we got to the bridge over the brook, she stopped, turned, and said, "No talk of communism, or socialism, or dictatorships. These men are from the Party."

I was not thinking about the men. At school, I sat on the back steps to do homework during lunch. The girls looked and turned away. I heard them repeating the letter *Z*, until their voices sounded like bees buzzing, as they said "Zofie."

The skinny man, Comrade Franta, walked in the fields, strolling, his hands behind his back. He went down the swale. I could see him near the brook on his knees looking for something. He came back with leaves fanned in his hand. He wore a hat with a feather in the brim and walking boots, even though he still had on his rumpled suit. Sometimes he alarmed me. I'd be in the barn looking for Nedda, who'd gone missing, when he'd come around the corner, his long legs jerking like stilts.

"Guten abend gnädige Fräulein." His eyes twitched with amusement. "You are studying German," he continued. "Perhaps I can help you?" As he spoke, he loomed over me. I could not tell if Comrade Franta was making fun of me. He inhaled his cigarette until the ash glowed; his eyelids blinked open and shut. He dropped the filter on the ground, watched it burn for a second, and then crushed it with the toe of his boot.

"Ich kann nicht Deutsch sprechen." But, as I spoke, I was

surprised I could say a sentence after four years of taking German at the Leninski.

"Aber ich kann dir helfen," Comrade Franta said in a lilting voice, "German needs to be studied systematically. The language reveals rich themes in literature. You cannot allow yourself the anger Czechs feel about the Nazis. German is an old language. You cannot expect to read with depth unless you master German."

I looked up at him. His suit jacket hung from his shoulders, his head was tilted, his eyes glimmered, he smiled. I did not understand what he meant. I did not want to be close to him and I could not confide in Uršula, could not tell her about the offer for lessons; it would confuse her. She became tense around the men. She'd not allow me to be alone with one of them in the sitting room. She would not want them spending extra time in the kitchen nook. One night when she and I served them dinner, the platter tipped, a dumpling rolled into Comrade Jakub's lap. He laughed, picked up the dumpling, and slurped it into his mouth. Uršula blushed, handed me the platter, and disappeared into the pantry. She hated mistakes. The next morning, her voice faltered when forced to inquire how they wanted their eggs.

The men demanded coffee, bread, another helping of pork. Behind their backs we called them by their given names. Dinner after dinner we cleaned saucers of cigarette butts, napkins stained from Jakub mopping meat from his chin and beer foam from the milk mugs.

Upstairs, every night, Franta smoked as he paced in his felt *valenkis*, the soles shuffling on the creaking wooden floors.

One morning before the sun was up, I woke to the sound of someone singing. The song was a Bohemian forest song, one of my favorites from music class. It was Franta singing. His voice filled the house, melodies rose and fell, stirring the quiet of morning. Each word he sang hung in the air singularly, beautifully, like a bell in a church. His voice was clear, in tune, sad. At the same time, I smelled the thick, nauseating smell of stale cigarette smoke that filtered through the vent. Franta was in bed, probably in his pajamas, smoking, as he usually did. He had never sung before. Jakub was still asleep; I could hear the rumble of his snores fill the pauses of Franta's songs.

After Franta finished his song, the house seemed empty. Uršula was now up, in the bathroom before me, to tidy up after the men from the night before. At breakfast I didn't mention the singing, nor did she. Maybe, I thought, I had imagined the sounds. When Franta stopped singing I felt alone, I wanted more. The next morning Franta sang again, and every morning thereafter we were woken up with Czech folk songs or forest songs.

I was feeding the chickens. I was reading in the sitting

room. I was walking home from the train station. I was hanging clothes on the line. And there appeared Franta, arms crossed, standing in a doorway, or at the end of the road, or looking at me out of his window.

"When you are ready, I can help with German," he said, shrugging his shoulders.

Uršula heard from the grocery store owner that the priest from St. Jost Church was transferred to another village and that a younger priest from Slavonice had taken over. The director of the Leninski Skolni left with his wife. A manager of a food collective was now working with the local manager to reorganize distribution and crop collection. I told her that two new teachers replaced two others in the lower school. One Monday, as I arrived at the train stop on my way to school, five farm boys I'd seen in the village over the years were on the station platform, with flimsy suitcases, ready to get on the Prague train, going there to live and work—as I knew others before them had—in an armament factory.

"The State," Uršula said, when I told her about the boys.

One morning, three girls in my class waited for me at the gate. Our grades from the first tests had been posted. I had no desire to look at my grades. I turned to go back down the street, to wait in the side alley until the bell called the girls to class, but this time, Ludmila, the leader of the group, broke away from the others and in a high, strained voice said, "Zofie, you got the best grade!" The other girls came up and shook my hand. I was suspicious, wondering what they might have in mind. Ludmila looked at the other girls and then looked back at me. "Maybe you will be invited to come to my house on Saturday afternoon," she said.

There was a package for me on the kitchen table. I had never received a package before. The only packages were labels for Uršula's jam jars. Could it be from my real mother? The older I grew, the more I wondered about her. I was young, four or five, when I somehow knew that Uršula was not my mother. I had no way to imagine what my mother or father could look like, and no way to have feelings for them, but the fact of the difference I felt around Uršula made nights long, and in dreams I was lonely, walking on winding roads that didn't end, or waking up just before my mother was to appear. Perhaps, I thought, after all of these years, I'd learn about her. Uršula was out, doing chores. Who had left the package? Should I open it alone? If my real mother were sending me something, why would that something arrive like this? Why would she have waited so many years? I pictured an album about her life, photographs of her that looked like me. I unwrapped the string and removed the brown paper. It was a book, not an album, not a box of letters written by *her*.

I turned the book over and read the title: *The Redhead*, by Johannes Richter. On the cover was a picture of a boy with freckles and bright red hair. The book was translated from German. On the back a paragraph explained that it was a story about a boy no one understood.

Jakub's car pulled up to the house. I slid the book under Jakub's newspaper. Franta knocked on the kitchen door. Without waiting for an answer, he walked in. His eyes fell to the packaging paper. "You've found the book," he said. "We can talk about it when you are ready."

I had never read an entire book, only excerpts in textbooks and parts of books that we read in class. One had to be fifteen to borrow books from the library. Other than a Grimms' fairy-tale book, there were no books in our house. Until I sat down later that afternoon and listened to Franta tell me that Johannes Richter wrote about how he had suffered from being made fun of as a child, I had no idea a writer could explain feelings that felt as if they were mine.

"We can have a lesson," said Franta one Saturday when Uršula went to visit her old friend, who was now dying. I gave in. I did not want Uršula to know, so we met on those Saturdays in the parlor on the two chairs by the tile stove. I sat straight, held my legs together, kept my hands folded in my lap; Franta leaned back in his chair, his legs were crossed at his ankles, his caterpillar eyebrows furrowed, his hands carved the air as he spoke. The lights flickered off in electrical outages, the wood I had fed into the fire hissed. Franta and I spoke in German. He corrected my grammar and gave me short lectures about literature.

"Beliefs change, books endure."

In slow, precise, simple German, he told me about characters and scenes and love and hate and beauty in the books and stories by Leo Tolstoy, and how Tolstoy at the end of his life sought simplicity and spiritual clarity and how he died on that unfulfilled quest in a train station. He explained that Émile Zola gave the French working class a place in literature as he was the first writer to offer his heroes a point of view about life in coal mines, lives lived in poverty, and in factories that employed children. Franta promised to bring books that were classics, translated into Czech, that needed to be read multiple times. He commented that a *poor* person is one who cannot imagine life beyond his own door, and that education was a gift in life as it was something that could never be taken away. And he said there were certain moments in a life that can only be relived or understood while one reads. Franta's eyes sparkled when he mentioned names of books. He told me about his niece Annetta, her polio, her life spent on her back in a sanatorium in Lausanne those first years before she could wear braces, and how his sister read her *Heidi, Le Grand Meaulnes*, and *The Little Prince*.

The Redhead was more than I could read in one sitting. It set off associations. Every night I reread what I had read the night before and then started the next few pages. I felt I was betraying Uršula and our life in her house by reading, as I was being transported to places I had never imagined, places Uršula could never have understood, places she'd never care to think about. I visualized the characters—the difficult mother, the fat father. I felt how Johannes suffered because of being gangly. I could imagine how the group of boys in his neighborhood made fun of him, and how they had no idea how alone he felt.

At school the girls were as distant as before: they didn't call me names anymore but no one invited me to her house. They continued to talk as if I were not there. I tried to break into their conversations, but realized I had nothing in common with them and nothing to add. Since this school was in the next town, I didn't know anything about the girls' families.

Now that I'd left my first school, I didn't see old classmates. Eva had been a friend. Her father owned the little grocery store, and we had walked there after school to see if he would give us candy. A few times she gave me discarded Polish TV guide magazines her mother liked to read. I hid them in my room as I knew Uršula would not approve. The one time I brought Eva home for tea, Uršula said, "Now off to play outside, the day is sunny." I wanted to show Eva my stone collection—the pink and blue pebbles I kept in one box, the striated small stones in another—and the stack of drawings I'd worked on, of houses I imagined I lived in. And there were the cutout photographs of women from the TV guide magazines hidden in the back of my cherry wood armoire. I took them out at night and wondered, was the woman with blond hair leading a Polish folk dance my mother, was the young woman in a tight red dress in front of a backdrop of shimmering cloth my mother, did the woman with the auburn curls in an advertisement about shampoo look like my mother?

In October I began to get headaches in class. The first time I felt faint, I asked to be excused. The geography teacher instructed me to go to the office and lie down on the cot. The secretary, Pane Havel, typed while I rested. At last I felt well enough to sit on the edge of the cot. Pane Havel twirled her chair so she could see me. She said that probably these headaches would go away in a year or so, and that sometimes girls the ages of twelve and thirteen get them. She told me about when she had them and how her mother would have her lie down on their living room sofa and how her mother would close the curtains and put a wet towel on her forehead. She also told me how the period of time with the headaches reminded her of when she was younger and used to have tantrums. She had no idea how they began, what triggered them, but after screaming and kicking while her mother tried to soothe her, she could not escape the feeling of being trapped in them. Her memory reminded me of the tantrums I had also endured.

Once in the summer, during one of those Bohemian hot spells, when I was in the kitchen and Uršula was upstairs, I heard her open and then slam the door to my room and run to the top of the stairs. She yelled down to me, "You moved the bed. It should not be under the window. That was Milan's room. Never change anything in this house. Fix it now." Fury ignited inside me. I ran up the steps and passed her, opened the door, and suddenly yelled. I turned and looked at her and yelled again. Now I knew I did not belong in this house. I was not even free on a humid night to sleep under the breeze of an open window. As I yelled, Uršula held her hands over her ears, and then she said, "Fix it now." When she returned later and found me hiding under the bed, she said, "Get out from under that bed. You can't stay there all day." She grabbed hold of my ankle and pulled, but I held onto the iron bed leg. Soon she was pulling the bed and me through the room.

"Leave me alone," I said. I was embarrassed by my behavior. The strength of my voice, and the sensation of feeling the pent-up emotion rise through my body and come out of my mouth alarmed me. Thereafter, the smallest complaint from Uršula would set off these rages. She yelled at me and threatened me, saying she'd take me to an orphanage if I did not start to behave properly. I didn't want her words to control my anger or even soothe me. I didn't calm down until Uršula finally left me alone. During one of the rages, Eva's father happened to stop by to ask Uršula for her next installment of jellies. He must have heard me crying upstairs. I overheard Uršula tell him how I sometimes acted impossible. She said moods had to be controlled. I should not think I could upset her routine with childish behavior. My door was open. Eva's father was on the landing below. I heard him say, "Leave her alone. It's hard enough she can't control herself. The tantrums will stop in time."

How did he understand that? I had only spent afternoons with Eva at their house. I had hardly seen him. Uršula followed his advice. The next time I fell into one of those spells, she came into the room, seemed ready to try to scold me out of my fury, but then left, shutting the door—not slamming it as before, but pulling it quietly until it latched behind her. She stood outside as I whimpered. I could picture her: arms crossed, ear cocked to the door, the floor creaking as she shifted her weight. Five, ten minutes she stayed, and then she marched down the steps.

One day at school I felt a headache coming on. I was in

the secretary's office lying on the cot. I told Pane Havel I had an appointment in an hour with the doctor. She accepted my excuse and signed me out early. It was a relief being outside the plaster walls and narrow corridors and away from the girls. The air was summery, clouds drifted over the fields. After the train, I took a shortcut through a farm. Whiffs of weeds hurt my head. Waves of dizziness made me lie down on the grass. I propped my head on the school bag. I thought about Johannes.

In the book, Johannes did nothing right. His father told him he'd never be normal because he had red hair, knobby knees, and big ears. Johannes knew he was clumsy. He tripped when he ran, dropped his books, spilled his soup, forgot to shake hands with his parents' guests, had no friends, looked out the window, and daydreamed in school. But what I liked was how he noticed birds. Birds preening, birds migrating in late summer, birds nesting in trees outside his window, birds alone on telephone wires, or flocks of birds taking off from fields all at once, their wings dipping and rising.

Johannes wished he had come from another family, wished he had a father who would have kicked the ball with him or taken him fishing, not a father who sent him to his room because he chewed with his mouth open. Lying in the field, with the book alive in my mind, I heard birds chirping, pecking at seeds left from the harvest. I forgot about my headache, got up, and went home.

The sound of a raised voice from the second story drifted across the garden. Startled, I took a moment to recognize that it was Uršula's voice coming from her bedroom. I hid in the shadow of the chicken coop. The window was open. A quilt, as usual, was hanging from the sill, being aired. I heard the mournful sound of a cow mooing from the neighbor's shed and then Uršula's yelling, "Get out! Get out of my room! I'll report you." I saw her dart across the room.

"Uršula," a man's voice—Jakub's voice—said in an irritated tone, as if she were a child and not obeying. "Come back downstairs. I just want to talk to you." Uršula's shoes clattered on the floor, running, I imagined, to lock the door.

"Come down, please. I'm not going to hurt you."

I guessed Jakub wanted to be with her. I thought of the subtitles of what the handsome man said in the Polish television soap opera I once saw at Eva's house—"I want to love you because you are beautiful." But what did love mean?

I crept into the kitchen, through the hall door, and up to my room. Uršula, now alone in her room, was crying. I could picture her on the side of her bed, her hands covering her face.

That afternoon something was different in her expression. When I came downstairs, she did not look at me.

"My head hurts," I said.

Uršula never talked of illness or pain. She did not trust

doctors. She made herb teas, boiled mint as a remedy, made broth from beef bones. She opened the door even in winter for fresh air. When she heard my complaint, she said she'd bring me soup. I went upstairs, shut the door, and closed the curtains.

I couldn't stop thinking about how I had heard Uršula cry, and how her voice seemed cupped in her hand. And Jakub. In some ways I could understand why she'd not want to have him as a lover. He had hairs growing from his ears, hairs coming out of the collar of his shirt, and he always chewed with his mouth open, but over time I'd gotten used to Jakub. He was heavy, big boned, his face round and red, head bald, beard trimmed. On weekends, Jakub wore a vest and woolen knickers. He sat under a plum tree and looked over what I assumed were his work papers. I liked watching him there, how he slouched in the chair to allow the sun on his face. Now, all I could think of was the mole on his cheek and how he made Uršula upset when, I guess, he was trying to show her love.

After dinner, after hearing the men rise from the benches and the kitchen door shutting after them, I came down the steps. My head pounded with each step. I held onto the bannister. I was afraid to look at Uršula, afraid to find her more broken than she'd been in the afternoon. She did not notice me. She sliced a piece of bread halfway through, then stopped and stared at the counter. She broke two eggs into a bowl but seemed to have forgotten why. She paused and stared at the counter again. She picked up the knife and walked into the pantry. She came back out a moment later and wiped the knife she had been carrying on her apron.

In the next few days, she didn't wear ironed blouses. She had bags under her eyes. She moved with less deliberation, cowering in her mood as if under a shawl.

One evening about a week later, when I was in the parlor doing homework, I could overhear a conversation in the kitchen.

"Uršula," Jakub said in a stern but soothing voice, a voice that made me realize that something had changed between them. "You must come with me to the Baltic Sea. We will take a train. You will see fields and woods. You will see towns. The tracks will go by a small river as the train travels north. We will walk on the boardwalk along the beach. We will have coffee with whipped cream in an outdoor café. You will see seagulls darting and flying over the waves. You will feel fresh air and like the smell of salt. It will make us happy to be at the seaside."

"No, Comrade Jakub. Water scares me."

"And the sound of the waves on the beach. You will see."

"I have work. I cannot think. I cannot dream."

That night I heard footsteps. Jakub went back down to

the kitchen where Uršula was ironing. It was late when the door of the bedroom opened and then closed. The following afternoon when I was taking out the pail of garbage, I found plastic packaging of a girdle in the incinerator.

In time, Jakub's attention made Uršula stand straight, walk with energy, she began to wear lipstick. She'd pause at the mirror in the front hall, take out a stick she kept in a pocket, rub the end over her bottom lip and then use it as rouge on her cheeks. She hemmed her plaid skirt to her knees. She wore her polished heels whenever Jakub was around.

"Where's Uršula?" Jakub yelled up the steps to me on one of the Saturdays when she had gone to Mesto. It was after my lesson with Franta and now I was finishing the last of *The Redhead*. The world around me disappeared as the story pulled me in. Dusk had fallen, and because it was a rainy afternoon and I had already turned the bedside lamp on, I did not notice how dark it had become. I became aware of the ticking of the clock and then the click when the hour hand passed six o'clock—the time the alarm was set for in the mornings. It was late and normally either I'd be helping with dinner or I would hear Uršula in the kitchen. I rolled off the bed, slipped on my shoes, ran down the steps to find Jakub in the dim light of the kitchen, buttoning the top button of his raincoat.

"Maybe the train was delayed," he said as he grabbed

the flashlight Uršula kept on a shelf. "I'll walk to the station to see." The door shut, and before I managed to turn on the path lantern, he was swallowed by the darkening night.

He cared about her. He cared more than anyone else, including me. I wanted to care, but I didn't know how to show that. I felt left out. I did not belong to her. She told me she was not my mother. She told me I probably would never know who my mother was. Before she did not talk to men. She had never asked questions, never asked for their help, never wondered why they had been assigned to her boarding house. Did she love him and not love me?

She was curt when she addressed those she knew, as if she thought the fewer words she used, the less confusion she might inflict. I can't think of a time before Jakub when she spoke up spontaneously, other than when Eva's father stopped by to see if she needed anything. Occasionally, she stated rules or made comments or asked me questions, but she was never curious. When I had asked her about her family, life in this house, having a younger brother, she furrowed her brows, and stared at me as if I had intruded on something private and distasteful to remember.

This evening was the first evening that Uršula was not cooking dinner. The house felt lonely. There were no sounds of the cast-iron skillet being put on the stove, or the chopping of vegetables, or the creak of a rolling pin. I was rarely encouraged to make a decision about dinner, but now realized that Franta would be coming down, and when Jakub and Uršula got back from the station something should be cooking. I turned on the lights, placed kindling and a log in the stove, and set the table. As I was filling a mixing bowl with flour and baking soda to make biscuits, I noticed a crock-pot in the pantry. In it was a stew that Uršula must have prepared in the morning. Where could she be? I found myself worrying. I had never worried about her. She had never been late, never done anything that did not fall into her rigid pattern of chores and duties. What if something had happened? What would happen to me?

Franta came into the kitchen. He looked around, shrugged his shoulders and seemed to also feel the absence of someone he had relied on without perhaps ever thinking she might one night not be there to attend to him.

"How long has Jakub been gone?" he asked when I told him that Jakub had left to meet the delayed train. Franta settled into the chair by the window. When I served him a beer, I became the maid and not the student. I had nothing I could say to him even though I was almost finished with *The Redhead*. I could have thanked him for this first book. But at that age, for me anyway, it was hard to show appreciation for something that I had not expected.

By eight, the stew was bubbling, rain was pounding on the

roof, Franta helped himself to a second beer from the icebox. I tidied and wiped and dried dishes and folded dishtowels.

"Shall I serve you?" I asked. Franta moved to the table with his book and beer stein.

"I wonder what the delay is," he commented as I placed a bowl steaming with carrots, potatoes, and meat in front of him.

"It has never happened."

"Well, they will be along."

After a while we heard voices outside. I ran to open the door to find Uršula leaning on Jakub. He had his arm around her, propping her up. They were drenched and shuffled inside, he a bit before she. Her cotton bag hung and dripped from his shoulder.

"Bring a chair."

Franta rose and helped Uršula settle in. The wicker back creaked with her weight.

I peeled the plastic raincoat from Uršula. Her hair was matted with a clump of dirt. She shivered. Uršula never showed vulnerability, was never cold or had a chill, nor was she hot or tired or frightened.

"What happened?" asked Franta.

"Later," said Jakub. 'Let's get Uršula comfortable." Jakub handed me his coat. He knelt, removed Uršula's shoes, helped her stand. He led her to her room to change. Franta and I watched as they left the kitchen. On the stairs, I heard Jakub tell her to take one step at a time. From downstairs, I heard drawers in her room clatter open. When she came back she was in a dry blouse and fresh skirt. I served the stew and biscuits; it was the first time I had served Uršula. When Jakub got up to get himself a beer, he came back to the table with Uršula's shawl, which he wrapped around her shoulders.

"A hot meal," said Jakub. "Just what we need."

After dinner he helped Uršula onto her feet to take her back to her room. When he returned he said, "She claimed she got dizzy before she slipped and fell. I went to the station, she was not there, and when I came back via the brook I found her. Nothing seems broken."

After that and all winter long, Jakub doted on her. He brought her chocolate powder, lamb shanks, sage spice, peppercorns, and a carnation or two when they were available. I heard them talking at night while she ironed.

"You went where?" Uršula asked.

"You made goulash this morning?"

"You came back through the woods on such a foggy night?"

"You pruned the roses and didn't ask my opinion?"

Outside the kitchen door, Jakub chopped kindling while humming. He helped mop the floors, he told stories about growing up with his grandparents in a little village in Moravia: the endless snow that fell all one winter long, skating on the pond, smells of his grandmother's bread baking.

"We are all orphans," he said one night when Uršula offered that her parents and brother had died from consumption.

In early spring, Jakub and Franta were moved to another posting in Caslav. Uršula's whistling, the lightness in her gait, plum cakes, breakfast cider—vanished. Boiled potatoes were plunked onto the table for the next set of apparatchiks. Her beet soup was lumpy; pork was sawed rather than carved. Underpants and undershirts were simply plucked from the clothesline and deposited on dressers. Uršula spent late evenings sitting by the unlit fireplace staring into space. She had sewing in her lap but only stitched if she heard someone coming. For a few weeks she forgot to make my lunch. When letters came, she did not ask me to decipher Jakub's slanted handwriting, but took them to the postmistress in the village.

At school, Katarina, one of Ludmila's friends, approached me when I returned after the week I stayed at home. I'd never paid much attention to Katarina. Now Katarina walked alone down the path when she spotted me, she said, "Are you all right?"

I never knew what had changed, why someone would become my friend. Was it my singing? Did they get used to me? Did they forget about my homemade-looking clothes?

Was it that I was now wearing a uniform? Katarina and I sat near each other in class; we shared our lunch—she liked Uršula's little salami sandwiches and chocolate biscuits, and I wished I had salad in a plastic box with the boiled egg sliced on top. We walked to the train station together. Her house was twenty minutes by train in one direction, my village, half an hour in the other. Those first days when I was just getting to know her, I dreamed I could look like her with her short blond hair, straight teeth, and her smile. I couldn't ever be her; my hair was reddish and thick. I had a gap between my teeth. I had freckles.

A few weeks before summer vacation, Katarina invited me to her cottage on a lake in Moravia. Perhaps because three boarders would be coming to our house and one of them would use my room, Uršula gave me permission to go. Neither Uršula nor I wanted to share a room. I didn't want to hear Uršula making her sleeping sounds and she thought it wasn't good for my eyes when I read in bed.

I fretted about what to take. We didn't have a suitcase. I didn't have new shorts. I'd never spent time with a family. From reading, I learned that people came from long family histories, that who your grandparents were mattered. No one at my school knew where I came from. They didn't know that even I didn't know. All I knew was that Katarina spent summers with her grandmother. Her father worked in Plzen, her brothers went to school in Brno. No one ever asked about me.

Katarina and her brother Tomas met me at the train. I blushed when they came up to me. I'd never been around a boy. They looked so much alike that at first I was confused. Were they twins? I knew they weren't but I couldn't get over how their smiles and eyes and expressions were so similar. Katarina wore a skirt and a pink-checked blouse. She was tan, her hair was wet as if she'd just gone for a swim. I felt rumpled and was embarrassed by the cloth suitcase we bought at the collective, but they didn't seem to care or notice the rusted buckles or the ripped seam.

Tomas, evidently excited to drive now that he had just gotten his driver's license, steered the car recklessly down the road. His door flew open on one curve. He laughed and pulled it shut. We drove past fields, the windows were opened to blasts of hot air. Katarina fiddled with the radio, but there was only polka music. Katarina and I were sharing the front seat; half of me was pushed into the door. Tomas turned off the main road onto a country lane, the car bounced on ruts, I braced my hand on the dashboard.

Tomas slowed the car. He turned into a lane and then came into a clearing. We stopped in front of a wooden cottage set between two pear trees. Katarina reached across me to open the car door.

"We'll get your bag later."

The cottage had two stories and a porch that looked out over the water. We entered into a kitchen where there was a table crammed with cheese, bread, and pickled fruits.

Katarina's grandmother—with her white hair, handsome face, and sparkling green eyes—stood on a footstool to reach the stove. She held out her arms and waved for me to come to her. She shook my hand, looked me in the eye, and said, "Call me Maticka."

"Here," she said, handing me a paring knife. "Are you handy at peeling? My grandchildren are good-for-nothings, swimming, sleeping late, lying around all day reading."

"No, Maticka, that's not true," Katarina joked.

Katarina took the knife from me. "First I'm going to show Zofie around."

What caught my eye were the bookshelves in the living room, in the bedrooms, even in the hallway. I learned later that there were novels and biographies and books on philosophy that were written in German, French, and Czech. Some books were new, most were old. Some of the covers were crackled. Some of the French ones: *The Coming of Age*, *The Little Prince*, *Simone Weil: Her Life*, had creamy colors with faded red lettering. Some of the German ones: *The Magic Mountain*, *The Sorrows of Young Werther*, *The Critique of Pure Reason*, *The Glass Bead Game*, *The Tin Drum* were bound in tan leather. The books were not stacked vertically, as they were in the library at school, but were horizontal, or tilted, or haphazardly placed on shelves.

Katarina said, "Most important is the lake." We went through the garden and down an overgrown lawn. In the distance, fields spread to hills that rolled into faraway mountains. The sky seemed immense and blue. We walked out onto the dock, the water was calm. At least it looked calm. I had not yet told Katarina I didn't know how to swim.

The first morning, I woke early and went down to help out in the kitchen. Maticka—in an apron, her hair in a loose braid—was standing on her stool, making dough for coffee cake. I handed her the cinnamon and sugar. She was surprised that I knew how to butter and flour the tins. She handed me the silverware. She got milk and honey from the icebox, sliced some cheese, and folded last night's napkins to use again. A sharp sound of a car backfiring startled her. "The older boys," she said, "coming in from Plzen." Doors slammed. One of them, Ptyr, knocked on the window before coming into the kitchen. Jiri, the other brother, gave Maticka a long hug, lifting her off her feet.

"You're squeezing my bones," Maticka said, smiling.

That night after dinner, Tomas suggested I help him wash the dishes while the others played cards.

"After I finish patching a leak on our boat, I'll take you

and Kata for a ride." The plates clinked as I carried them to the sink. I had never been on a boat. His voice was quiet, unimposing, inviting. I didn't know what to say. Would I know how to balance when getting into a boat? Would I feel scared being surrounded by water? Would they all decide to jump overboard to take a swim and expect me to follow? I pictured myself twisting awkwardly before landing in the water and sinking like a stone to the bottom.

"Yes," I said. "I would like that."

"I'm done." Maticka laid her cards onto the table. "Tired back, tired feet. Time to put the brittle bones to bed. I'll be lucky to see the sun come up."

"You'll outlive us all," Jiri said.

Looking at Maticka, at the light in her eyes, her gnarled hands that lifted iron pots, her attempt to conceal her smile in her own amusement at her life prediction, I thought, "She will outlive us all."

Later, Katarina and I went to the dock. The brothers were smoking and drinking beer. Waves licked the wood pilings. Tomas passed Katarina his cigarette, and after she took a puff, she gave it to me. I held it the way Franta had, with my wrist cocked, tapping it. I put the end to my mouth and drew in a little smoke before quickly blowing it out. I looked from one brother to the other. They were talking about books being censored, about pamphlets they had been making, how a friend was kicked out of the university, about a demonstration where police used tear gas.

"I've joined a samizdat. We're going to start self-publishing prose in a few weeks. We've got three typewriters now," Jiri said. He took a piece of paper from his pocket. "Here are a few quotes from the last pages of *Steppenwolf.* Hermann Hesse, a German, wrote it. We've just translated it." As Jiri read, as he breathed between words, I listened. I heard his intonations as he spoke. I was not sure what he was really saying, but I got that it was important in some way.

"Time and the world, money and power should belong to all people. To some, to the sensitive man, there is hope." Jiri turned the paper over. I could see he had underlined the next part. He continued, "I say to myself: all we who ask too much could not contrive to live at all if there were not another air to breathe outside the air of this world, if there were not eternity at the back of time: and this is the kingdom of truth."

"Yes," said Ptyr. "If Hesse were here now he'd know that he'd not be able to breathe the air we are being forced to breathe."

Were they talking about Czechoslovakia? Communism? Someone like Uršula? A country controlled by obedient men like the boarders. The obedience that makes those like Uršula fearful of going against rules. I was not sure. I'd never thought how words might have to be erased or hidden, or about words that could become codes, codes the Communist Party was suspicious of and would arrest people for using.

Jiri said, "Think of banned books, imprisoned writers, writers beaten because they spoke out. Think of writers cowed into silence. The quotes we will make copies of will give us solidarity."

In what folded into Katarina's summer routine, she and I spent mornings lounging on the old steamer chairs on the porch overlooking the lake. We sipped tea while Katarina read passages from her romance novel about Ivan, the boy who had fallen in love with Ilana.

"This is too much," she said, and she then read a scene about them kissing: "Ivan held Ilana's hand and led her to the back of the kitchen. Once there, hidden in the shadow of an open door, he put his hand on her back and brought her body close to his. She arched her back, rose up on the tips of her toes, and pursed her lips. He kissed her for a long time as she felt herself melt."

A few days before, Maticka had recommended that I read *Frankenstein* by Mary Shelley.

"If as a child you read the comic strip of *Frankenstein*, this is now a chance to read literature," Maticka said.

She told me how it was a story about a scientist, Victor

Frankenstein, who creates another man by sewing limbs of various dead men together until another being is born out of the misshapen form. Victor is lonely and wants a friend. He had hoped this new man—who ends up being gawky and frightening to look at with his yellow skin that barely covers his veins, his nose, and his ears—would fulfill his need. But the new man is not only misshapen and large, he too is unhappy and even lonelier than Victor had been. He haunts Victor by showing up when Victor had thought he could not be found. Finally, the new man, as if confused about his identity (was he himself the man who created him, or who was he), bludgeons Victor to death. I could not sleep well those five days I read about the surreal creature fashioned out of bones, out of boredom, in an experiment. Why had Maticka suggested this horrible tale? Why was it so gripping that I couldn't put it down?

"Maticka," I said, "Why would a writer make up a character who is unhappy?"

"You do wonder. It's the wondering that makes the reader engaged. There's no answer but you will keep looking for one. The story stays. I read it forty years ago," Maticka said.

One afternoon Katarina and I walked beyond the high meadows to a stand of pines where there was a wooden shepherd's shed. The shepherd's wife made cheese, bread, and tea to sell to hikers. Sitting on log stumps around an upturned wine barrel, Katarina and I talked to the old woman. She was bent over, wore a peasant's apron, and had a long gray braid that she'd take hold of and then twist into a bun. She told us about being alone in the cabin for days when her husband was out with the sheep, how the wind howled through the trees in windstorms, how she was scared a tree would fall on the shed. She told us to be wary and not walk on the eastern trail. Dissidents and sometimes men as big as monsters hid there.

"Who are they? What do they look like?" we asked. She wouldn't tell us.

"Men?"

"Women too."

When the shepherd's wife wasn't looking, Katarina took the last pieces of bread from the bread plate and stuffed them into her shirt.

"Let's see if we can find someone, maybe that person is hungry," Katarina suggested after we said goodbye. As soon as we were out of sight of the shed, Katarina veered off the main trail and cut over to the eastern trail. What did dissidents look like? Maybe a man who wore a cape, or women hiding under a bush while writing stories? Maybe it would be one of Jiri's friends who wore a Beatles sweatshirt and was against communism and was running from the secret agency.

"Do you think a dissident is tall and has long limbs he

cannot control?" I asked Katarina. Katarina did not know I was talking about Frankenstein's monster, whom I kept thinking about because after he was created, he was ashamed about his ugly body, his ignorance, and his innocence. As we crept through the woods I imagined finding a similar monster—one we could tame maybe, one who would eat the bread and accept that people were nice.

But we jumped when a branch broke underfoot.

"I hear someone in the gully."

We held our breath.

"Run," Katarina said when crows in the tree above us suddenly began to caw. We fled down the path, panting, screaming, laughing, and finally, once out of the woods and in the open meadow, falling down in exhaustion.

One afternoon while Katarina, Tomas, and Ptyr had gone to the dock and I was alone on the porch pretending I wanted to stay to read, Maticka called me into the house. "Here," she said, handing me one of Katarina's old bathing suits, "put this on. It's time you learn to swim. I'm going to take you to the shore where we can walk in."

The beach was in a cove around the bend from their house. We could hear the others—the boys diving and cannonballing from the diving board, Katarina pleading with a brother not to dunk her. Maticka stepped out of her smock, dropped it on the grass. Her bathing suit, stretched from years of use, hung like a sack. She walked into the water up to her knees and looked back. I followed, not sure of what was going to happen. The sun was high and hot, the water cool around my knees. Suddenly, Maticka sank into the water, turned, and stayed afloat by supporting herself on her arms. She began to kick. "This is how we start," she said, "with kicking." I'd seen toddlers pretending to swim like this in the creek near our village. They looked like crocodiles with their legs floating behind. Now here I was with an old woman, crocodiling in the shallows of her lake. Flashes of her white thighs surfaced as she kicked. She blew bubbles and said I should do the same. I was relieved no one was watching and, at the same time, relieved to know that Maticka knew that I didn't know how to swim. After a few moments of this exercise, she said, "For the rest of this week, we're going to take this slowly, an afternoon at a time."

She walked deeper into the water, waved for me to follow. Soon we were waist deep. I held my arms out to the side for balance and took small steps, feeling the mud, the slimy water plants, and a stone underfoot. Maticka waddled over until she was standing behind me. She put her hands under my waist and instructed me to drop into the water, into her arms. I did not understand what she meant, but once I dipped in, she put one arm across my chest and the other across my waist, and lifted me up. I was weightless.

"Now kick," she instructed. "Blow bubbles. I won't let your face go under."

I was reluctant to roll over, afraid of water in my nose. She took a few steps as I flapped and kicked.

"Okay," Maticka announced after ten minutes or so. "You will get waterlogged if we stay in the lake too long." She held out her hand so I could get back to my feet. We waded to shore, she handed me the towel. We stood side by side and I watched our wake ripple until it grew calm.

After the third summer that I went to the lake, Franta came back to board for a month. It became clear that he had something to do with administration in schools in Bohemia. He'd been at the Leninski during a few mornings, meeting with the director. One night before dinner he made one of his appearances. I was outside reading on the back step when he came up to me and said, "Zofie, you are now sixteen. I need to tell you that the tests you did well on in June make you eligible to go to the Oty Pavla Gymnasium in Prague. Your scores are good enough to have school and lodging expenses paid for by the State. It is arranged that you can stay with a couple near the school."

It took a while for me to understand the offer. Reasons for not wanting to go confused me. But then Franta explained how I'd be preparing for university in Prague and for a career. I thought of conversations with Katarina's brothers at the lake and books that I had read there. I had a vision of what my life might become: working in the village school library, helping Uršula with the boarding house, working in a store. "I would like to try the school," I said to Uršula when Franta brought up the subject of Prague after dinner. Her voice quavered as she said yes, and then she turned and went into the pantry, the place of her emotional refuge.

Though I had visited the lake house with Katarina for the last three Augusts, I had never been invited to their house near Plzen. I had never met her father. Her mother, Kristina Vacek, had come to the lake now and then. She wrote high school biology textbooks, always seemed to be working, and had little free time. I did not feel as comfortable with her as with Maticka. Katarina's mother was pretty. Her hair was flipped into a twist, and she wore a scarf and linen skirts and soft leather shoes. But she seemed agitated being at her childhood summer home at the lake. She snapped at her mother for making fattening desserts, and spent most of the day on the porch with stacks of papers she was working on. She never asked me questions.

When Katarina's mother was not there, I spent time in the kitchen making dumplings, washing lettuce, and talking to Maticka, but when her mother was there, I felt like a maid.

I was not educated or refined. I was still learning manners by watching Katarina and Maticka. My clothes came from secondhand stores. Katarina's mother greeted me the first day we met, but she appeared distracted and did not look me in the eye. At times I felt her regarding me during dinner, and wondered what was I doing wrong? Not putting my glass down in the right place, not sitting up straight, being too quiet when others were talking? I sensed that Katarina—when around her mother—might have felt awkward to have me as a friend, and I imagined she was embarrassed by how her mother was treating me.

I had never noticed how Katarina was really her mother's elegant daughter until her mother arrived. They both sat with one leg crossed over a knee, swung that leg sometimes, pointed a foot. They were confident of little things: opinions about books they had read as children and ones Katarina's mother commented on, or remembering the years when friends came from Prague for the weekend, or how it would be interesting to invite the local apparatchiks to show them what country cottages were like. It was a side of Katarina I had never seen. What I noticed was how Katarina's mother did little things like take long puffs of her after-dinner cigarette, lift her chin, blow plumes of smoke over her shoulder, and then lower her eyes as if to express disinterest in an ongoing conversation.

I watched Katarina watch her mother, and I could see how she admired her, and how she wanted to be admired, but her mother did not compliment Katarina about how she'd become calm and smart, or about Katarina's ideas to redo the garden, or about how she'd come to care about the household. But Tomas and their mother, it seemed, had the most connection even though they argued about books. He wanted to become a journalist. Their mother was disparaging about writing of current events. He had written his thesis on Franz Kafka, and wanted to talk about the characters, the predicaments Kafka's characters wandered into where they grappled with ideas of fate and choice.

"There is enough surrealism in our lives today, why dwell on it from the past," said their mother.

"Yes," said Tomas. "But I think surrealism is a sort of truth. Kafka's tie to his parents represents repression. Kafka asks where does he, where do we, fit? The similarities between then and now are interesting. I think many of his themes focus on the lack of freedom to dream."

A weekend came for me to visit Katarina's house. Katarina and her father, Otto Vacek, met me at the train station. He shook my hand, took my bag with the other, smiled, and said, "Welcome."

As he escorted me, with his hand on my back, guiding me to the car, and then holding the door open—Katarina insisted I sit in front so I could see the countryside—I was introduced to a kind of man different from Jakub and Franta. Here was a man who knew how to make others feel comfortable.

"How have you liked visiting the lake?" he asked. "I hear you've a scholarship to go to school in Prague," he continued, and then he told me how I'd be charmed by the spires, the Gothic arches, and the Baroque churches.

"You'll make the most interesting friends," he said, as if remembering his own past.

When we reached the house, I felt shy and in awe. The house looked like a creamy yellow castle with molding over the doors and windows. I could not believe I had known Katarina for three years and she had never talked about the grand, beautiful house she lived in. If she had, I would never have felt worthy of being her friend.

Katarina and her father jumped out of the car, her father grabbed my suitcase, we walked up the steps. The front hall was as big as Uršula's house. Stone steps curved into a second and third story. The furniture was dark, couches and chairs were covered in faded red, bookshelves went across and up walls in one of the rooms and filled an adjoining nook. The dining room had a long table. Katarina pointed at the glasses in an armoire and told me that their family had been in the glass business for almost a hundred years. Vacek Glass Works had been taken over by the State, but her father managed the factory in Plzen.

By the time we were upstairs, I began to see the rooms with Uršula's eyes. Everything was messy or faded. Three centimeters of dust floated under the four-poster bed in which I was to sleep, flowered wallpaper had peeled from one wall, curtains sagged from the rods, floors had buckled, the sheets on my bed were unironed. At home, though we had only two armchairs with hard cushions, a sitting room with four wooden chairs, and the kitchen table with benches, everything had always been wiped clean. Every day Uršula dusted and mopped and threw the bed covers onto the windowsills to air. A pitcher of flowers was on the counter, her jelly jars shiny on a shelf, linen hand cloths creased and in piles.

"My mother hates housework," Katarina said as we came down to the kitchen. "When she's around, dishes sit in the sink for days. It's just as well she's not here this weekend, as we'd have to do everything."

That first night, Katarina, who had a headache, stayed on the couch in the sitting room watching television until she finally, after dinner, went to bed. I stood in the corner of the kitchen, feeling awkward, watching Tomas measure rice as his father reached into the drawer for silverware.

"Here, Zofie, use this peeler. You more than anyone know how to cook."

I laughed. Tomas told his father how he and I had helped Maticka, how I had made lemon cake, and about the picnics we'd had in the cove last summer when he grilled venison sausages over the fire.

That night he and his father and I made paprika tomato sauce and filled green peppers with meat and onions. I chopped carrots, celery, and parsley. Tomas and his father talked about the latest student protests, when the police clubbed two students until they passed out, and how all phones were now being tapped in the university district of Jinonice in Prague. I liked how his father annunciated words in a rhythmic way and how he looked at me directly as he spoke. In an unutterable wish, I imagined him as my father.

After dinner, Tomas asked if I wanted to go for a walk. I did. I wanted to see the park around the house. The air was cool after the sun set. We walked out through the remains of an old garden. Tomas explained that during the war three German officers were billeted in the house. His father's parents, newly married, had just taken over the house from his great-grandfather, but were obligated to stay in the maids' rooms while the Germans lived in the bedrooms on the second floor. His grandmother refused to talk to the officers, refused to look at them, and when asked to clean their rooms, she never changed their sheets, never cleaned the sink after they shaved.

"Everything fell into ruins. Year after year, an exterior wall, the garage paving, a staircase chipped, peeled, or simply fell apart. And no wonder," Tomas said, "nothing has been gained all these years. Communism resists beauty and civilization."

We walked the length of a wading pool that was filled with linden leaves. One remaining linden loomed over us—the only tree thriving in the garden. At the bottom of the garden, stubs of sculpture pedestals poked through the long grass. A breeze blew leaves across the lawn. We walked around a wall and looked out over the fields.

"It's all a collective now," he said. "What my great-grandparents owned is no longer ours. No one complains, no one can say anything."

We circled the house, walked past impressions of old gardens: a boxwood maze of tangled branches, an orchard of ghoulish, rotten-smelling apple trees.

"Come this way," Tomas said. He went through a copse of trees. "I'll show you something interesting." He led me through thick undergrowth, holding up a thorny bush for me to duck under, warning me of a low branch. I stepped into a hole and fell and was embarrassed that I had groaned.

"Are you all right?" Tomas asked. He helped me stand.

My shirt was caught in brambles. Suddenly we heard something, a branch break, a dog, someone, something breathing hard. Tomas took my hand, held it still as a way to tell me not to move. We waited, the breathing got louder, but a breeze blew through the leaves and we couldn't hear anymore.

Then when the wind died, lightning bugs filled the dark. Tomas led me, still holding my hand. We came to an overgrown graveyard. He continued, we walked around the graves. All of the graves had the name Vacek on them. Two were newer.

"What was the noise?"

"I don't know," he said. "A dog. Someone lost maybe."

"Does it scare you?"

He turned toward me. His eyes were dark in the dim light; he put his arms around my shoulders and hugged me in a brotherly way, in a warm way. "It should be nothing to be scared of," he said. Then he stepped back, and motioned for me to follow.

He left me at the house while he went to the village to see if there were reports of anything unusual around the neighborhood. The house was quiet when I went upstairs. I found Katarina's door shut, only one light was on in the bathroom at the end of the hall. I wondered which room Tomas slept in, if he slept in a wide, high bed like the one in my room, if he fell asleep while reading, if he kicked the eiderdown covers off in his sleep, if he hugged his pillow.

I savored the luxury of a bath. The water was soft, the sound of its running filled the room, until I turned it off and there was a silence that was more silent than before. I leaned back into the perfectly shaped porcelain tub. I lathered soap onto my arms, my shoulders, my neck. I stayed under the water as long as I could, feeling in one way alone in a strange, grand, crumbling house, and in another way safer than ever.

The address of the couple with whom I'd stay in Prague as a boarding student for the new school had been sent by Franta. I had instructions about which trams to take to get to their apartment, and the registration for school was tucked in my pocket. Uršula and I took turns carrying my suitcase to the train station. She puffed, her feet wobbled in her heels.

"It's heavy," she said. "You're taking books after all."

The only time I had ever left Uršula was during those summer weeks at the lake. I had never said goodbye to her. Would Uršula and I hug? Would I give her a kiss the way Katarina's family did when they came and left? I had never kissed Uršula, she had never been affectionate with me. Waiting for the train, Uršula reached into her pocket and took out an envelope.

"For you," she said, and pressed the yellowed, glued paper folded around some money into my bag. Then she held out her hand for me to shake.

"Send news." She was wearing her lipstick for the occasion. Her hand was waiting, suspended. "Don't forget me." She wiggled her wrist. I took her hand in both of mine and kissed it. She blushed, stepped back, sighed, and watched me as I lugged the suitcase up the three steps into the train and walked down the aisle to my seat. She waved until the train left and I could no longer see her standing in the station.

By the time I found the tram in Prague, my shoulder ached from the weight of the suitcase. I reached the Malecks' apartment house and a man with one arm greeted me.

"Pan Maleck," he said formally and, without looking into my eyes, he took my suitcase. He leaned near the wall as he walked, his empty coat sleeve hanging. This part of the limestone apartment building looked onto the river. Clotheslines were strung from window to window. My room, a maid's room near the kitchen, had a broom-closet-sized WC.

"You may shower on Tuesdays, Thursdays, and Saturdays. You may use four minutes of hot water." Pan Maleck pointed toward a timer on the shelf of the main bathroom.

Though it was raining the windows were open.

"It is Friday," he said, "the day for fresh air." He unlocked the living-room door with a key and pointed to the corner at a television covered by a lace cloth.

"Saturdays you can watch television. We have dinner on Sundays.

"Beta," he continued, forgetting formality, "is an administrator in a woman's hospital in Trebon. She's home on weekends."

I unpacked quickly, folding my shirts and putting them on the one shelf over the narrow iron bed. I noticed how the blanket was tucked, the flat pillow, the low bed, and I slid the suitcase under it, next to my other pair of tie shoes. There was a bedside table and a child-size chair by the window. I pulled back the filmy cotton curtain and let light into the room, wishing I had a key so that Pan Maleck could not come in when I was gone. There was only a small mirror in the bathroom, no toilet seat, the sink water dripped.

Gray streets, large buildings with tall windows and balconies, and trees along the avenues—limp from rain—were my first impressions of Prague. A man crossed the street with a newspaper covering his head. Chairs were stacked in front of cafés, but sounds of men drinking, arguments, and laughter came through the doorways. I walked and walked, mainly in circles, and was sure a young man I noticed down the street was Tomas, or a young man walking with a woman was Tomas. It rained all afternoon into the night.

I woke up with the chills, drifted back to sleep. As there was only one blanket, I pulled my clothes off the shelf and piled them on me. The following morning, weary from shaking, I realized that because my coat was still wet, and it was still raining, I would not be able to leave the apartment.

Beta Maleck was in the kitchen. I expected a double of her husband. Instead, she wore slim slacks, and had a pleasant smile. She was a shorthaired, knobby woman with parchment skin.

"Coffee?" she asked, and then said, "Just call me Beta."

I'd never had coffee but didn't refuse her offer. She added milk. It was bitter.

"It is a fact," she said as if we were friends, "that I travel too much. I get so tired. I go to Moscow to the pharmaceutical conferences; I stay in dormitories for administrators. I'm too old to sleep with other women I don't know. In Trebon, I share a room with two nurses. We have use of a kitchen." She cleaned as she spoke.

"Come," she said after collecting my coffee cup and putting it into a plastic tub of soapy water. We walked down the hall to the sitting room. The door was shut, but not locked.

"This is how you turn on the television. How you change the channel. You may use this room on Saturdays. My husband works in his study on weekends."

I sat down on a tattered chair and looked at the television but did not turn it on. There were no books, just a shelf with small porcelain dogs and other figurines—the kind a child might collect.

Beta puttered. I heard the broom swishing in the hall, the mop in a bucket. Later, she appeared in the sitting room to dust.

"You must not always be here. You should not do too much homework. You should go to museums, go to swim at the Centrovat, go to parks, be with friends."

In time, I ventured out from my neighborhood, strolled through the Old Town onto Parizka, and wound my way through the narrow side streets to look at cafés, galleries, and stores. I crossed the Charles Bridge and wandered along the Mala Strana. I discovered parks, tiny vineyards, and paths up the hill to the Hradčany Castle. I took trams to neighborhoods, and tried to imagine what it might have been like had I grown up in a city rather than in the countryside. I walked along the river on Malostranska to look at the formidable apartment buildings. On beautiful days, the city was bright; the sun gleamed on the water. On winter days, when fog clung to buildings, it felt as if everyone had weights in their souls. The Charles Bridge was black from smog, soot covered the fading paint on the Baroque buildings, cats ate garbage in the gutters. Every morning, shops selling Polish clothes opened at nine, faded awnings of cafés were rolled out, stooped women swept with twig brooms, and students sauntered to Charles University.

I found a job as a waitress on Sundays in the Café Slavia. The pay was not much, but I liked the activity of people drinking coffee and having conversations. I used the money to buy shoes, a wool coat, underwear, hair bands, hand cream, and a bathing suit and cap for the swim class that the gymnasium required students to take.

While serving soup or salad or tea at the Café Slavia, I overheard students talking about how they had to be careful when they tuned their radio to American or English rock music. "I came back to the dormitory one day," a young man said to his friends, "and the radio was gone, my school papers had been rifled through, drawers were left open." A German woman who came in often for coffee said to her companion, "Beware what you include in your stories. Any embellishment of life in capitalist countries will be rejected and confiscated by the Party." In another conversation an older woman said, "We need more translated literature. We live in an intellectual vacuum."

At school, in the mornings, the classmates I got to know greeted me with friendly handshakes. I joined in the conversation at the lunch table. Sometimes we sat around after school and talked about boys. Sometimes three of us went shopping, which was really more of an excuse to walk around together, stroll into stores, and pretend we had the money to buy the coats or hats we tried on.

Back at the apartment, I buried my mind in books, and spent Saturdays at the desk in the sitting room. The tones and words of other languages resonated by threes; Akhmatova, Akhmadulina, Yevtushenko; *eaux, ruisseau, rivière*; *lieben, lesen, lachen*. Names, nouns, verbs. I made lists, filled note cards, memorized the literary verb tenses, looked up meanings in my dictionaries. That year I read a short story by Platonov in Russian for Russian class, some of Kafka's stories in German class, and George Sand's letters to her son in my French seminar. What if *The Redhead* had not been translated into Czech? I would never have been able to read him when I was thirteen. Nor would I have read Mary Shelley or all of the translated German books we read in European literature class.

Uršula called from the post-office phone. "Zofie, is that you?" It took her a while to trust that it was really me on the phone.

"There are more apparatchiks," she said. "They stay too long. They bring beer. They drink all night in the garden. They swear. Cigarettes overflow ashtrays. They are having a phone line installed here sometime this fall."

A few months later she called to give me the telephone number.

"You will not believe it but I am talking to you from the pantry. The phone is on a shelf next to the flour. Are you still there? Can you hear me?" Without waiting for me to respond, she went on, "I've fixed up the two-room shed into a room. For me. Eva's father made the other small room into a water closet. Now, I will rent more rooms. Are you there?"

I wanted to ask her about Jakub. Had he ever reappeared? And Franta?

"Unless you're in a hurry after work, have a beer with us," said a girl I had waited on. Her name was Tereza. I sat down after my shift and she asked where I studied, offered me a cigarette, poured a glass of beer out of the tall pitcher. I took puffs of the cigarette, inhaling shallowly, afraid I'd cough.

"I don't know about you," Tereza said one night after I'd been included for a few weeks, "but I think the lectures at the university are so tedious."

I nodded, wishing I was old enough for the university, not just attending their summer courses.

"Are you taking French? I'm failing," Tereza said.

I offered to help, and soon we got together once a week. She had a dream of going to France.

"Paris. I'm going to live there some day. My grandmother used to sing songs to me in French."

Tereza told me that she loved music, and one afternoon, when I was walking her back to her room after our French hour, she steered me down an alley just off of Clementinum. On the corner was a small, soot-covered church with a handwritten sign: Konzert 16:00 – Chopin. "It's free," Tereza said. "There are free concerts all over Prague. You just have to learn where they're given."

I started going to concerts alone. I began to recognize faces in the audience—an old couple who smiled at me, a group of schoolgirls who stood on the side. I often sat next to a woman at the church concert who told me about the performers. The music made me nostalgic for Uršula. I missed her and our minuscule life—the two of us in her tidy house, the sounds of the radiator, the whistle of wind in winter, the rooster crowing, the clank of fluted jars of elderberry jam and forest mushrooms as Uršula stacked them.

After a choral recital in a small auditorium in the Rudolfinum, I wandered over to the Kampa Gardens. There I saw Tomas for the first time in what seemed like forever. He was with two girls and another young man, two of them on a bench, two standing, having what seemed to be an intense conversation. It had been a few years since I'd seen him last. I'd been to the lake house with Katarina the summer before, but none of the brothers had been there, and this past summer I had not been invited. Katarina and I were not in touch for some reason, but I kept thinking about Tomas. I often thought about that night on the parched lawn, remembered walking to the graves, the woods when he took my hand. Now he was wearing a turtleneck sweater and jeans, his hair was long, tucked behind his ears, he had a goatee. He stood up from the bench, reached into his back pocket, pulled out a booklet and began to read. His friends laughed, one of them ripped the booklet from his hand and riffled through the pages until he found something, pointed, and then laughed again.

I sat, watched, was unable to move, hoped he'd look my way, hoped that if he did that I would be able to raise my hand into a wave. Soon the group broke up. He walked side by side with one of the girls. I followed them to the end of the street. They grew smaller, dodging between pedestrians.

The next Saturday I returned, thinking they might have a routine. I came again the following week. Only an old man feeding pigeons was on the bench. I wrote to Katarina, asked how she was, what she was up to. How was her grandmother? Her brothers? At last, a tattered postcard of a church in Brno arrived.

"I have a boyfriend," she wrote, "and a job in a greenhouse. Come see me."

Six months later I saw Tomas again. He was leaving the Slavia one evening with two friends.

"I can't believe you're here, Zofie. You look great. Have you heard from Katarina?" he asked.

"Not for a while," I said, "other than a card inviting me to come sometime."

He looked at me as if considering who I now was. "Are you free to meet me here next week, say Sunday?"

All week I could not concentrate. I had an exam in Russian, which I had to pass, which I did with Pan Maleck's help. I had no idea what Pan Maleck's job was or what he had done in the past. He could be one of many walking to work, hunched, his one arm swinging, working in a building that I imagined was full of cubicles, working with people who followed rules, people who were afraid to say anything that went against the grain of communism. At home he lived for his music. Violin concertos filled the apartment. Evenings he worked—doing what, I don't know—in the sitting room at the desk. Weekends, when Beta was at home, he closed himself into one of the bedrooms. I never saw that room or their bedroom. Their lives, like the sitting room and the dining room, were locked with his key. But he spoke Russian and, like Franta, helped me with homework, reviewing declensions.

Tomas arrived late in the afternoon after my shift. I was self-conscious, sitting at one of the tables, turning the pages of a book. My fellow workers looked at me, as if wondering if I'd been forgotten. Then Tomas came in the door with a book bag hanging diagonally across his chest, his hair wind-blown, ragged jeans trailing over his tennis shoes, his eyes searching the tables looking for me. I waved.

We sat and waited for the beer he ordered. His left leg was restless. I remembered that about him. How he rarely sat still, was always ready to get up and do a project.

"Tell me about Maticka," I said to break the awkwardness.

"She's getting old. Her arthritis keeps her in bed. She can't see well. She falls."

"And the others?"

"Well," he began, "I spent three weeks at the end of the summer at the lake house, trying to fix a corroded pipe, scraping paint. I replaced slats on the dock. I'll need to go back to finish. And what else? Jiri's working on a second degree, he wants to teach literature at the university level. Ptyr is coaching a state hockey team. Oh, my parents are estranged. They were arguing incessantly. I could not be around them. They didn't seem to want to make an effort. It makes everything about our childhood seem like a lie. What was the point of their even getting married if they can't figure out how to have a normal conversation? My mother stays in one side of the house and hides when Papa is around."

I waited for him to tell me about Katarina, but he took another sip of his beer and looked out the window.

"And Katarina?"

"She says she wants to get married. That's what is strange.

One marriage dies and another is about to happen. Maybe both marriages are for the wrong reasons. I think she said it would be in a few months. You knew that, right."

I knew nothing. I felt lonelier than ever. Katarina getting married, but we were so young.

"And you, Zofie? What are your plans?"

"I'm thinking about getting a degree as a translator," I said, almost a bit surprised at hearing that come out of me. "I love the feeling I get when I'm reading in another language. It feels like music. The same feeling happens when I do translations in the foreign language classes I am taking."

"I wish I had language skills." He paused, then said, "Let's find a place to talk where it's not noisy." He poured himself the rest of the beer, drank it in a few swallows, motioned to the waiter for the bill.

We walked along the banks of the Vltava. Lamplights flickered. A policeman in front of the National Theatre shifted his rifle from one hand to the other. The air was refreshing.

"I'm in a samizdat press," Tomas said. "You remember how Jiri used to make copies of poems that might have been or had been censored." He turned his head and looked around, first down the street, then behind us. He put his arm out to let me know to slow down as we approached two men in long coats. He didn't speak until we passed them.

"I guess I'd like to be a person who is working toward that day when all will be told."

Later, sitting in a park, he rested his hand on my wrist as he talked about freedom of the press, how tragic it was that we Czechs were discouraged to think. My nerves were jittery but at the same time I was aware of a sleepiness, of being one of those Czechs who sauntered down life's predictable path. I had no great ambitions. I was like committee members, the apparatchiks, the secret police, the everyday Czech woman. I was afraid to make waves, upset the equilibrium. I wanted to be accepted, to avoid fear and intimidation. I thought that was all I wanted. But it was not all I wanted.

"Remember how Jiri and I talked about books being censored, that contemporary poetry is condemned as being anti-Communist?" Tomas asked. "I've joined a press to avoid going through the State publishing process, to avoid the inevitable rejection. We make copies of poems or stories and pass them around, and then those who read them make copies and pass them on. We've talked about getting them out of the country, to Germany, France, the United States. It would be more effective if they were translated.".

We got up and walked along the river. While Tomas talked, I paid attention to his words: liberty, repression, intellectuals, writers, ideas, energy, discipline, fortitude, vision, iron curtain, fear, freedom.

"If you're willing, here's how the samizdat works, how we do it. You use carbon paper to make copies of the poems or stories. It's best if you can type but if you've got good handwriting that will do. You work where no one will suspect your activity. I give you a few pages at a time or we have drop points with friends who will meet you at the park or in the library. You leave a folder on a bench or by a certain book if you are in the library. Contact people will take the translations out of the country and they will bring stories or poems to us to translate into Czech. It sounds like a lot of work. In a way it is, but you'll be part of our group, though no one knows who the other translators are so that everyone is protected from being caught."

Tomas continued and mentioned how playwrights, songwriters, rock musicians, novelists were followed, their phones were tapped, when caught they were interrogated, blacklisted, and often sent to prisons or camps. Some journalists had been beaten into submission. From that came fear of thinking, fear of one's own truth.

"Yes," I said. "I can try."

That evening he took me to the Café Savoy. We drank Hungarian wine and dipped bread into soup. He looked at me.

"It's nice to be with you again. You seem centered and studious and independent."

He walked me home. A storm was gathering. The black

clouds grew and crept across the darkening sky, a breeze shuddered in the trees, and from somewhere far beyond the city came the sound of thunder. Inside the door of the apartment building, Tomas kissed me goodnight on my forehead and then hugged me. I hung onto his jacket, holding him as he turned to leave.

"Don't go," I wanted to say, but the door clicked, the hall light blinked on. In my room I did not undress, I did not lie down. I sat in the chair. I had never felt Tomas's presence as much as this, not in summers on the lake, not that night at his family house near Plzen. I remained still, afraid that if I moved, I would lose this new feeling of being included in something important, something that would matter to others in a world larger than mine. And I might lose the feeling of belonging to Tomas that I had begun to feel as we walked along the river. From outside, a strange light lit the panes. I stood and opened the window. One shaft of lightning followed another. I looked at the silent street, the gray façades of apartment buildings that glowed eerily, beautifully, with each flash. I watched the silent lightning until the palest dawn diminished the flashes, until my feelings, too, dimmed, until I remembered his kiss had only lasted a second.

I picked up a folder of stories that was left in the Slavia with a waiter. These were to be translated into German. One was a fable, another was written as a stream of consciousness, another was from the point of view of a worker who loaded coal in a mine and was forced to work overtime, as he was slow. At night his wife soaked his feet in hot water. She did not tell him about her day: the "comrade's" fingers, being backed into a corner, the grizzly mustache in her mouth as the comrade bit around her chin.

I had to do the translations in a hurry; I never felt they were right, but there was not enough time for perfection. Tomas usually dropped them off at the Slavia, and for the following six or eight months he met me on Wednesdays on a bench by the river to pick them up. Once, as we were talking in the park, I asked him if I could read the thesis he wrote about Kafka.

"I have no idea where it is. I liked writing it. The strangeness of Kafka's world seemed to fit my somber mood that first year in university."

"I read *The Trial*," I said. "Maticka recommended it. I am not sure I understand why there was the persecution of Josef K. What was his arrest about? Why was he executed for a crime that was never named? Why did he feel guilt before he was arrested? Why did he cooperate?"

"It's complicated," Tomas said. "Josef K.'s quest to confront his destiny in the nineteen thirties is about the search for identity. He is a German living in Prague. In one way the story is about the uselessness of bureaucracy, which Kafka illustrates by having the character walk through the building of nameless offices, where one hall mysteriously opens up to the next, and where there are in fact no employees. It is a dead-end labyrinth which mirrors Kafka's despair about life."

One night, after he had suggested we have dinner together, Tomas kissed me again and gave me his usual warm hug, and of course a part of me yearned that once again something was beginning. He handed me a letter from Katarina and told me that he had to move to the lake, that he needed to disappear for a while, to take a step away from the samizdat. Someone had been following him.

"I'll be back soon I hope, Zofie. It'll be safer if we're not in touch for a while, but I'll be thinking of you. I look forward to seeing you again." And then he was gone.

Later that summer I went back to see Uršula for a few weeks. She walked with a limp now and said her knee was giving out on her. We sat at the kitchen table and peeled potatoes for my favorite *bramboračka* soup. The evening glow shimmered on the waxed wood and illuminated the tips of her white hair.

"Tell me about city life," she said, but before I thought of what she might like to hear, she sighed and said, "I'm getting old. It's hard to cook for these men. They don't help except when Jakub comes."

"He comes still?"

"In the fall," she said without betraying any emotion. "He works for hostels in southern Bohemia now. When he's here he prunes dead branches from the trees."

I pictured him on the rickety ladder, wearing his green vest, pipe in his mouth, taking orders from Uršula. Meanwhile she'd be wearing her low heels, collecting fallen branches, dragging the longer ones to the woodpile.

At first I was restless at her house. It was her house. Uršula was Uršula, not as warm as Maticka. I had grown up with Uršula, but grown close to Maticka. But after a day or so my mind quieted, the languages that rumbled around in my brain arguing with each other receded from my consciousness.

Before going back to Prague, I took the train to Brno to see Katarina. The train was stuffy and when I stepped out the Moravian summer heat hit me. I was immediately uncomfortable. The humidity, though, shimmered around Katarina. She put her arms around my shoulders and hugged with an affection I'd come to love. She smelled familiar, like fresh air.

"You must be tired."

She was wearing baggy cotton pants and a man's shirt

tied at the waist. "Work clothes," she said. "I've got a job at a greenhouse. Hard to believe that I'm already at work at age nineteen. I am already exhausted and I have to finish the planting I started earlier today." Her face was flushed. We got into her boyfriend's car and drove south from the city center, past wheat fields. Katarina drove fast, the car sputtered when she shifted gears and lurched forward from stop signs. We arrived at a farm collective where there were rows and rows of greenhouses. She told me she was tending the plants for the Moravian Communist Party Festival that would take place in September. She stopped at a gate, showed her identification and a pass she had for me, and then parked the car.

"I told them you were a botanist. That you needed to make some sketches."

I followed Katarina. It was hot outside, but the humidity in the greenhouse felt watery. I could feel my hair curling around my face.

"How do you stand this heat?" I asked.

Katarina began to move flats of vinca from one shelf to another. There were lemon trees and palm trees growing in plastic pots and flats of flowers with plate-size blossoms. There was a faint perfumed smell from the lemons. I looked up at the red flowers of one potted tree. The sun filtering through its foliage gave the leaves a papery transparency, the blossom was rubbery, fluted, and had a phallic-looking yellow stamen filled with tiny pores. I reached out to touch the rubbery red. It was so smooth it looked artificial; something about it was ugly, menacing, indecent.

"Don't touch that," Katarina said.

She was transplanting the vinca into bigger pots, digging a hole in the dirt and then carefully placing each plant. The vines caught as she separated them. She had to tear the tendrils apart.

"The stamen?" I asked.

"Any of it. It puts off a terrible odor. You can't wash it off for days."

I sat down on a box next to the potting table, and rather than seeing Katarina, I was sitting on a bench with Tomas.

"I should show you the sights," Katarina said after she had finished the watering.

"Sights?"

"You know, city gates, the façade of City Hall, Moravian architecture."

She drove aggressively through intersections, just beating red lights, and while parking the car in a tight spot, bumped first the car in front and then backed into the car behind. I was about to say something, but she appeared calm, as if this was the way one parked here, so I didn't.

"I haven't been here for ages," she said, dropping the keys into her handbag.

"Since when?"

Katarina didn't answer right away. She pointed at the row of houses in the alley.

"I met Georg here. We used to come on weekends to have lunch in a café. It was winter then, it was beautiful when it snowed, everything sparkled and looked clean. I remember thinking it was so lovely, that we should always come back, but we never seem to come here now."

"Why not?"

"I don't know, it just doesn't happen. You'll have to come back in the winter after one of the big snows. Then we'll walk all around and have lunch in the café and sit in front of the fire."

Katarina and I used to build fires on rainy days at the lake. We would sit on the hearth, poke at the logs, and then blow to get them to burn, while she folded pieces of newspaper and threw them, sometimes with perfect aim, other times missing and hitting me.

"Think of all those fires you loved making."

"Yes, and the ashes Maticka made me clean out the next day."

Now we were walking in unison, like soldiers on the cobbled street, our footsteps echoing in the narrow alleys.

We stopped in front of a house that Katarina told me dated back to the 1500s. A writer used to live here, Katarina said, but she couldn't remember the name. We sat down on a bench. Two linden trees leaned from the house into the street; a flock of swallows, chattering in the trees, formed a background of noise.

Katarina crossed her ankles.

"Guess what?" she said, but before I had chance to think of something she smiled and said, "I'm pregnant."

She was looking at me. I lowered my eyes, I couldn't take the power of her gaze, the chatter of swallows filled my ears. "It's the most wonderful feeling. You can't imagine!"

An odor of standing water wafted from the small fountain, and something else smelled rancid, something from a gutter, something nauseating, like a sewer.

"Really," I heard myself say. "That's so exciting."

"Georg doesn't know," she said. "It's only two months. I want to be sure, so in a week I'll tell him. He's Catholic. He'll be so happy. He loves little children."

"And you are getting married soon?" I asked, remembering Tomas's bitter feelings about marriages.

"He can't afford a wedding ring. We've talked about going to the civil office. It's no big deal. He doesn't want family there, says it should be just about us. I agree."

I gave her a hug. She threw her arms around my neck and squeezed me hard.

In a part of the city filled with cement apartment buildings, where Katarina lived, we spent the night talking, reminiscing, on a lumpy bed in a room she rented from an elderly couple. I was tired, a bit dizzy when I fell asleep. I did not meet Georg this time.

After a week in Prague and with still ten days until classes started, I was restless in the Malecks' apartment. I thought of Ettie, the character in the book I was reading, called *Iza's Ballad*. Ettie was afraid of the city, she mourned the past, she was trapped as an old woman in her daughter Iza's apartment. She spent her time watching a pigeon pecking on the window, as if wanting to get in. In a burst of loneliness, I called Katarina and asked if she could meet me at the lake. I knew that it would not be possible. Georg had left in the car for a week. She said she couldn't come, that I should get in touch with Tomas, maybe he was still there. She emphasized that I should feel free to go anytime. I left a message on the phone for Tomas, and told him how Katarina mentioned I could come, as I needed a break from the city.

Tomas was not at the train station. I had tried to call again but there was no answer. I took a train to the village and then sauntered through the fields, following tractor paths that Katarina and I knew well. When I got to the house, it was locked, the key hidden under a stone. He had left it seemed. After I let myself in, I noticed yogurt in the icebox and cheese on the table. It appeared as if he'd be back. Would he be angry? And if so, how would he behave? I wondered for a few moments until I realized that what was more disappointing than not finding him there was Maticka's absence. Wherever my eyes landed—the piles of plates on the kitchen counter, the rumpled pillows on the couch, the dusty windows—I felt as if something had been scooped out of my chest. My eyes watered. Nothing would be as it had been, and I was the uninvited witness to the passage of time.

I decided to sleep in Maticka's little room, which was now musty and empty of her belongings. At times in the first hour or so, moments of panic welled. It was not my house. It was wrong for me to have come, wrong for me to hope that Tomas—were he to return—would accept the audacity of my arrival. But the doubts faded. I felt at home in a way I had never felt. I had never been alone in any house, and now, for the time being, the space was mine. I began to organize the cottage, putting sheets on Maticka's bed. I opened windows, straightened pictures, returned books to the bookshelf, swept. Yes, for Maticka, I thought, but then something else occurred to me. I was always cleaning. I had learned from Uršula. Our life together was regimented by the daily tasks of housekeeping. Now I dust and tidy up wherever I go. I wondered if this habit—restless in nature, that seeks to fulfill loss or find perfection by rubbing away layers of dust and wax and veneer from something like an old trunk or table—might also stem from a hope of finding a trace of the past. Or was I trying to please someone? Or now, was it a way to feel closer to Maticka, the only maternal figure who had embraced me?

Later that evening, I tuned the radio to a piano concerto, settled into a deck chair on the terrace, ate the rest of my sandwich from the train, and listened to tree frogs chirping near the water.

With crisp air pouring through the window the next morning, I was startled to discover where I was, but then I was comforted by thoughts of Maticka. She had adored me, probably still did adore me. I'd visit her as soon as I could inquire where she was living.

As I worked all morning, I was aware of how Maticka had made me feel at home, how she had given me books to read and encouraged me to speak up at dinner by asking questions. Around noon—after cleaning nonstop since dawn—I remembered the day she had decided to teach me how to swim, when she had appeared on the porch with Katarina's bathing suit. I had been timid and fearful to expose how limited I was in life, how frightened I was of water. I had never expected anyone to show concern for me.

Once, a few years after she had taught me to swim, she came down to the dock where Katarina and I were lying in the sun, sat on the edge of the plank diving board, and said, "Okay, girls. Let's see you swim all the way across the bay." Katarina and I swam side by side while doing the breast stroke. When we returned, she said, "That was too easy. Work on the crawl. It's better exercise."

Thinking of that, I changed into my bathing suit, walked to the dock, dove in, and swam the bay with an ease I never could have imagined years ago. Swimming in the pool at the Centrovat had made me into a strong swimmer. It was wonderful being back in lake water. I wanted to drink the velvety liquid as I swam. I stayed in until I shivered. After two more days of swimming and relaxing, I felt fit, and while brushing my hair after swimming, I looked in the mirror and saw how my eyes glowed in my healthy complexion.

Thursday midday, Tomas's car chugged to a stop in front of the house. I jumped up from the kitchen table, thought of hiding, but before I could do anything, he came through the door I had left open.

"I left a message," I said as he walked in. He paused in the hall, not so much in confusion at my unexpected presence, but his eyes grew wide. He looked around and noticed perhaps the field flowers in a vase on the hall table, the clean windows, bread on the counter.

"The flowers, the tidy house, it's for Maticka," I said.

"What? Oh, Maticka, poor Maticka."

Then he appeared to come to his senses. "But why did you come? Not to see Maticka. I told you that I shouldn't be in contact with the samizdat group. Didn't you know Katarina would not be here?" He walked off to his bedroom.

"I'll leave," I said feeling ashamed. "You're right to be annoyed."

"No, you don't have to go," he said coming back into the living room. "Just give me a few minutes. I'm tired. I forgot a document I need for a meeting tomorrow. I have to leave again this evening on the 7:20 train."

I went to the dock, and swam. Later, lying on the dock, I dozed until I sensed a shadow blocking the sun, and looked up to see Tomas in his bathing suit and T-shirt standing over me.

"I'm going for a row," he said, "come if you like." The boat was still undergoing his repainting, patches of white filler spotted the pale green hull. I pulled a shirt over my bathing suit while he turned over the boat and pushed it into the water.

"Do you mind rowing?" Tomas asked.

I had become proficient over the years, but now, self-conscious, I was dragging the oars on some of the strokes. I rowed along the shore, past the beach, past a meadow.

"I've been sanding and patching this boat since I was ten. Perhaps it's a metaphor for something in my life," he offered.

On the way back, I rowed into the middle of the lake. A pair of ducks took off from the shore and flew overhead. I dropped the oars to listen to the flapping wings. Waves lapped the sides of the boat. Tomas turned to watch. The sun was low now. The water glistened. I thought to reach for the oars, but was calmed by the still air and mesmerized by the almost inaudible lapping sound. We drifted, both of us focusing on something beyond the boat, both of us in some kind of quiet moment. Of course I was thinking of him. Who knows where his mind was? Perhaps he was simply waiting for the ducks to return. Then, Tomas stood up, the boat wobbled as he pulled off his shirt.

"I'm going to swim back." He stepped onto the seat and dove in. I watched as his body was swallowed by the lake, and waited and waited, and found myself counting: five, ten, thirty, forty-five, sixty seconds for his head to break through the surface. During that long minute, the sun sank behind the hills and the lake became black. At last, after thinking I might have to dive in to look for him, he came up for air. He flipped onto his back and waved before he swam to the dock. Chilled, I picked up the oars and rowed. The wood creaked in the oarlocks. I followed Tomas to the dock and tied up the boat. In one great energetic movement, Tomas pulled himself up the ladder as water drained from his body. Then, surprising me, he turned to me and hugged me hard and whispered in my ear that he liked me so much but, but... He didn't know what the but was all about, but he was confused and didn't want to string me along. He wasn't ready, for what he did not know.

And me? I wanted to ask. My feelings? Would he ever consider what I wanted?

Pan Maleck was in the sitting room when I came back to the apartment. People were talking. He never had visitors. I went directly to my room, but he called my name before I shut the door and said I should join him. It was Friday, the hall windows were open for the weekend "fresh air," but it was still hot. Shirts and undershorts hung on the clotheslines outside of the windows.

When I walked into the sitting room, there was Franta. He stood to greet me, held out his hand as he took a step to reach me.

"Zofie," he said. "I wouldn't have recognized you." I was wearing a skirt, and new shoes. My hair had been recently well cut and was clean.

I knew that it was through Franta that I had this room and the funds to stay with the Malecks, but I was not aware that he'd kept up with news about me. I didn't trust why he was here. I had become less of a complying citizen and more aware about communism. As a child, the tone of communism was all I had. Now I was wary of authoritarian rule, apparat-chiks like Franta and Jakub and Pan Maleck overseeing every detail of life. I hated having to fill out a form to buy stamps, and I hated to have to fill out a form to buy something as basic as aspirin. It seemed overdone when indoctrinated soldiers in helmets wielding clubs marched into the streets to break up student gatherings. I cringed every time the loudspeakers on buildings blared announcements, especially during concerts in the Rudolfinum, when a violin solo was overridden by an announcement that on Monday, the street Kaprova would be blocked for a Communist Party parade.

In my first three years here, I had learned from other students. I had come to resent Party bureaucrats. Pan Maleck was one of them; Beta, too. Most apparatchiks I saw in cafés or walking on the street had the same complacent smirk, the same baggy suit, the same white shirt, the same thin tie, and as far as I could tell they never smiled or laughed. I gathered that the fear of being caught doing something wrong kept them subservient.

My life outside of the apartment was my own business, the short translations were my silent rebellion.

I had never asked for help, but through Franta's inter-est in me, education had fallen into my path. I had taken advantage of it. And here was Franta, standing in front of me, probably in the same rumpled suit he'd worn when he first came to our village, his eyebrows beetling as usual, his grin fixed, his arms crossed in front of his thin chest, his foot tapping expectantly. He had lost whatever warmth he used to offer in our lessons. He had lost more of himself over these last years; he was thinner, grayer.

"Your scholastic record is strong. It is noted you were elected to take the superior translation course. The Education Ministerstvo has noticed you. You will do well to accept a post with a summer apprenticeship. You can then be eligible for housing funds at the university next fall."

I had my savings of 200 *koruna*. I was sure Uršula did not have extra money, and I was sure that my scholarship funds would run out before the completion of my studies. Without waiting for a response, he continued, "Committee member Comrade Milan Kucharczek will expect you." He dug his hand into his pocket and clinked his change. The conversation was finished. He handed me a typed address. I nodded thank you, we shook hands.

In my bedroom, I felt claustrophobic; the walls were close, the ceiling low, the bed filling most of the space. Without unpacking, I grabbed my bathing suit and towel and headed out to the Plavecky Centrovat. I took two trams to get to Letenske. Walking the last blocks there, I began to miss Maticka. I wondered if I'd ever see her again and realized I had not asked Katarina or Tomas where she was living.

At the Centrovat, I swam laps. The pool was not crowded, so I lingered; I got out, rested, then dove back in for another ten laps. I showered for a long while as it was the only place I could take a luxurious hot shower.

I was pulling on my shirt when I heard my name being called and turned to see one of the girls who'd been with Tomas and his friends a few times.

"Zofie," she said again, "I'm Maia. We met first in the Kampa Gardens. Do you remember?" She was short, had straight hair cropped to her chin, dark eyes. I remembered how she and her boyfriend were holding hands one afternoon in the Café Slavia, how she laughed.

"Would you like to have a tea?"

We settled into a banquette in the café at the entrance of the Centrovat. I was hungry and suggested we have soup. After we ate, she began to tell me about her writing, how a friend of a friend in Paris had asked her to submit a poem to a literary journal. She needed it translated, remembered that I used to translate for Tomas's samizdat, and now she was wondering if I could translate her poem.

"What's it about?" I asked, amazed that she could be so open with someone she didn't know well.

"It is a poem about a poor mother and her children on a special outing. What they suddenly see." She paused, as if shy, and then said, "I have the first part right here. It's not long. It's not that great but I have to send something. How about if I read it to you? It's always helpful to read aloud."

"Please do." I looked around, wondering if anyone would notice.

"You'll notice how my Czech syntax is a bit off. Just pretend I have poetic license to experiment."

Maia rummaged around in her bag, found some hard candy and offered me one, and said, "It's better to be doing something while listening." She opened a folder, took out two handwritten pages, and cleared her throat. I was immediately struck by her diction, how each word led to the next, unfolding the story of a gypsy woman washing clothes, of her singing, her children playing. In two short syllables, Maia made the sound of stream water rushing. She repeated lines of the woman's song. Allowing her words to float in my mind, I could hear the arrival of thundering hooves as horses and riders cantered into the nearby field. In the next stanza the cantering grew louder, got closer. In Maia's Polish accent, I understood the sound for thundering. I could picture the gypsy woman standing up, her song faltering, as she and her children observed in wonder: six boys and a mother on horseback, dressed like young counts and a countess. The syllables lilted as Maia read, "velvet helmets, black boots, laughter, blond hair, ribbons streaming from bridle brow bands, bits clinking, hooves on hard earth," and then after they were gone she finished her last stanza with words about the quiet, the stream rippling, the melody of the gypsy woman's song.

Maia tucked the poem into its folder.

I didn't know what to say. I wanted more. The mothers, the children.

"How did you ever come up with that?"

"From a dream."

As we stood to leave, Maia said she'd make a copy and meet me the following week after swimming so I could translate it. I was already thinking of the words in French, how the sounds might work, and the verbs. And I was thinking how these characters appeared in Maia's consciousness one night in a dream and were now etched into mine. But it was the mothers that intrigued me. I could visualize them: one in an old skirt with a red kerchief over her head, the other in a soft sweater, riding breeches, her blond curls bouncing. Could either have been my mother?

Midweek I went to the Education Ministerstvo as Franta suggested. The offices were in a post-war cement building, the windows fogged with grime, the corridors long, the doors closed with numbers on them rather than names. I looked at a glass partition and noticed a row of assistants, people my age and older framed between stacks of paperwork, all with stern, hard faces. Comrade Kucharczek shuffled out a door down the hall, his shoes scuffing the linoleum, a folder in his arm. We returned to his cubicle.

"You want work at the Ministerstvo. A summer internship, followed by course work at Charles University, which the Ministerstvo will prescribe for you, that will prepare you for the translation of textbooks."

I stared at him and began to shake my head without realizing it, until I saw him looking at me.

"A translator needs knowledge of vocabulary, a sense of systems, to understand trends in communism. Most books are in Russian. Some come from East Germany. The task is to translate words and phrases without losing the Marxist-Leninist ideals."

He leaned back in his chair, and rubbed his hands together.

"In the reception area you will find forms, an application for dormitory residence, rules, disclosures of commitment, disclosures of confidentiality."

I ran down the stairs, through the courtyard and out into the street, thinking that if I translated something like Maia's poem that suggested the pleasure and display of wealth, everything could change. I might end up back with Uršula, or spend time in a rehabilitation camp. I could lose a chance for further education. Or I could choose the expected path, could get the living stipend to study, to do translations for the Ministerstvo.

I hardly slept those next nights. I had no one to help me think this through.

I went back to the Ministerstvo two days later, spent hours filling out the forms, and was given a room of my own in one of the residence halls near the university.

At the Centrovat, I waited for Maia, ready to tell her that I could not help her. I took my time brushing my hair, avoiding my conflicting reflection in the mirror. When she didn't come to the dressing room, I waited by the café. I was eager to ask her about the two mothers in her poem. Were they modeled after her mother?

My heart churned with worry about confessing to Maia that I was a coward, especially in light of my thoughts about the strong women in her poem. After an hour or so passed and she still had not come, my head began to hurt. It occurred to me that something might have happened to her. After waiting another hour, I asked other swimmers and finally heard that Maia had been forced to go back to live with her parents in Bratislava after being called in by the university board because of the "subversive" tone of voice she evidently used in articles she'd written for the university news bulletin.

The translating I'd done for Tomas's samizdat had been about stories he deemed interesting. I could still feel the flow of Maia's poem inside of me. The children riding, the surprise the gypsy woman must have felt as she watched something happen that she'd never have expected or imagined. Was it possible in a socialist country to have a rich family still ride their horses in the countryside? Is a dream made into a poem reprehensible? That thought made me wonder how such a simple request from Maia to translate her made-up story had become a turning point in my career choice.

During the second summer of the translating job at the Ministerstvo, as a reward perhaps, I was given published Russian stories to translate. Not Chekhov or Gogol, but obscure Ukrainian writers who wrote the Party line. The themes were fixed; there was no color, no imagination, no moment with a description of nature. The plots were about work in a factory, moving up the assembly line to management, a good family, work on a farm collective, work in daycare centers. Any hardship had promises of a better life for all. The message for the stories printed in magazines and newspapers was "Work hard, expect little, don't be proud or have ambitions." Advancement, cravings, and capitalist consumption left little for the next man—your friend, your compatriot—and in the end exemplified the ruthlessness, the utter shame of the greedy.

I was entrenched in a métier where there was no mention of art or music. Now, in 1988 Prague, plays and jazz concerts were beginning to emerge from the underground.

Small bands preformed on terraces of coffee houses or in the Kampa Gardens. Handmade signs for homemade plays being given in church basements were tilted against back-door church doorways. At the Ministerstvo I was working in the remnants of the old system. One evening I went with work friends to one of the first free jazz concerts given at the university auditorium, but we were disappointed with the music, with the dissonant sounds of the overused horns. Yet the audience went wild. When we decided to leave early, fearful of police deciding to "calm" the enthusiasm, I recognized how instilled I was with fear, a fear that I became aware of when Maia had not come back to the Centrovat.

When Tomas came to Prague on weekends from his latest job in Tabor, I saw him a few times since I started my work, but he was always with a group of people at the Café Slavia. He was friendly, quick to give me a kiss, introduce me as his great friend, squeeze my arm, not knowing that he was setting off emotions that I'd been trying to overcome. One sighting of Tomas, or a conversation with him, stirred me for days and made my mind spin with scenarios where we were together. I sensed that he regarded me as Katarina's friend. I tried to talk myself out of my attraction, tried to rationalize that it was Katarina I adored, not her brother that I loved, that I was confusing the siblings.

Katarina wrote, saying so much had changed. Her mother had left her father for another man and had moved to a town on the border of Poland. Her father was depressed, her mother bitter. Maticka had lost more of her eyesight and had moved to a retirement home near her mother's new apartment. Maticka had left the lake house to her, Katarina, as the women in the family had always owned it. Her father still worked at the glass company, still lived in their country house, but because only he and sometimes Tomas were there, the Party forced him to let out rooms to teacher's assistants from our old school. Katarina now had two children, an infant daughter named Nataša, and a baby, Lukas. She was still living near Brno and invited me to visit.

Katarina's apartment was at the end of a narrow corridor. It had been two years since I had last seen her. When I walked in, she embraced me so hard I lost my breath. Her cheeks were flushed; her hair twisted into a clip, she was wearing her husband's shirt over wrinkled pants. There were only four small rooms for her family of babies and her tall, handsome sports-news-reporter husband. Like her mother, Katarina was no housekeeper. Toys were strewn about, diapers hung on a rack in the bathroom, the kitchen table was cluttered with open jars of crushed carrots and half-finished milk bottles. Katarina led me into the tiny living room, picked up Lukas, kissed him, and then gave him to me to hold. His arms were fat as sausages, his thighs chunky. He squirmed until I put him down and sat with him. Then he put his hands on my shoulders and started jumping and laughing.

"He's nonstop," said Katarina. "He even laughs at night when he's meant to be crying himself to sleep."

Nataša woke up from her nap and slipped into the room, hiding behind one of the three chairs by the door. Katarina held out her arms to her and soon Nataša was on her mother's lap, sucking her thumb, twisting a loose strand of Katarina's hair around her finger.

I am not sure we ever had a real conversation that week; there hadn't been time. Georg came home at seven, so hungry that he ate a bowl of cereal after a dinner of meatballs, dumplings, bread, and cabbage, and guzzled his beer. He bathed the children in the spit of a shower basin, pulled on their pajamas, read Nataša a story, gave Lukas a bottle, and settled them into bed. Then Georg watched hockey or soccer, drinking beer after beer. Katarina and I cleaned up the kitchen, folded diapers, and talked about the children, how Nataša was shy and Lukas so good-natured, about Katarina's friends who left their children in daycare centers, the shabby condition of those centers.

I slept on quilts on the floor in the living room. The first night I was fearful I'd never get to sleep, but somehow, as soon as I put my head on the pillow, I was dreaming. When I went out at noon the next day to buy fresh bread, the silence of the street in comparison with the demands of the children and Katarina's responsiveness—jumping up to get a toy Nataša couldn't reach, helping Lukas stack blocks, comforting Nataša when she ran into the side of the door, putting a dress on Nataša's doll—was a reprieve. Outside there were no immediate demands; no child crying that Katarina or I needed to attend to, no crash of a shelf that Lukas was trying to climb, no clamor of pots being pulled out of a cabinet in the kitchen. I lingered in a café and sipped tea; the quiet settled around me; there was only the clinking of teacups on saucers, the ring of the cash register, a low murmur of voices. After only twenty minutes, I became lonely, and wanted to get back into the midst of family chaos.

Georg never kissed Katarina when he came home, never asked about her day. Yet Georg's face brightened with delight when he held Lukas. He charged around the hall of the apartment with Nataša on his back, as if he were a horse, while she waved at us and commanded her father to go faster. He read to them, made them laugh when he pretended to be a clown. I was intrigued to see how a father treated his children. I hardly knew how to miss not having a father while growing up.

I felt appreciation for all that Franta had done for me, as he had quietly been a force in shaping my career, and for

Uršula and how stalwart she'd been to raise me. I had come to love Maticka like a grandmother, but I was in awe of Katarina. There she was lying on the floor holding up Nataša on her feet as Nataša let go of her mother's hands and flapped her arms, saying, "Look, Zofie, I'm an angel!" Or there was Katarina at the dinner table instructing the children: "Napkins on the lap, ask to pass the bread, drink the rest of your milk." Or at night, sitting on the edge of the children's bed on those nights Georg was not at home, holding first Lukas's hands and then Nataša's in hers as she said, "Now, pray as Pa likes you to pray. Say thank you God for everything."

The hours working for the Ministerstvo that summer after graduating from Charles University were endless. And soon one year was becoming another year. I slogged my way down the dawn-lit streets to the cement Ministerstvo building, sat at a table with the unlaughing souls, translated one word at a time, knowing I'd be checked, quizzed about the choice of words I made, forced to redo the document until it was correct by their reckoning. Because Franta had decided to make me into a project years ago, here I was now, an example of how a country child could be educated to a certain level and made like the others—the great socialist dream—my education a tool to perpetuate and illustrate equality. But beyond that, in the center of my being, I knew that translating literature was fascinating. From reading, I had learned how words portray emotion, how sentences and clauses lure a reader further into the characters' minds, how weather, interior scenes of houses, descriptions of people capture the attention of a reader. And since I was really no one, or so I felt, as my background was borrowed, or rather I was dropped into a scenario that I soon learned—thanks to Uršula's relentless honesty—did not belong to me, having a passion grounded me. When Tomas first mentioned his samizdat and the idea of me—with my studies in French and Russian and German—being available to translate the stories and poems he wanted to send around, it became a direction, then it became a career. Working on passages evenings when alone was my pleasure.

Day after day, I woke up in the apartment I'd moved to—this one was in the attic of a historical wooden building. The floors sagged, the windows were warped, and the thick plaster walls had warmth and character. I felt at last embraced by my living circumstances. I worked hard, came home exhausted, had little time for friends or for anything else other than reading and writing out my own translations of favorite paragraphs from Böll, Hesse, and Zweig into Czech. It was a way to slow down, to get closer to the writing, to feel a literary intimacy with the authors. Translating passages I loved reminded me of swimming in the lake; the sensation of diving in and being surrounded by clear water: my hair streaming, arms outstretched, body gliding in a soundless, expansive, dreamlike fluidity. Those smooth motions were comparable to the fluency of phrases floating in my mind.

Katarina called. She asked about work, about friends, and told me she wished she'd spent time in Prague before getting married. I wanted to know all about the children, how they liked their preschool, if Lukas was still so good-natured, if Nataša was still so shy. I didn't ask about her marriage, about Georg.

I yearned to hear news about Tomas. I learned he was helping Katarina with the lake house. She had no time to go there, especially because Georg hated the countryside and claimed his car was too unreliable to go long distances. I decided that the next time I went to see Katarina, I'd tell her about my feelings for her brother; maybe then I would absolve myself of those longings, maybe I would realize I was hanging onto a dream, maybe she would laugh and tell me just to be patient, that someone else would come into my life.

Ferenc, an editor in the department of translation, invited me out. It was the fall of 1989; communism was waning. The Berlin Wall had come down, and dissidents in Prague were speaking out, insisting on the freedom to act, write, play any kind of music in public. We felt the energy on the streets and it was all we talked about. Ferenc loved food and music and insisted on always walking. I became familiar with corners of Prague I had never known—small cafés, a sour-cabbage soup made fresh on Thursdays, dessert dumplings with poppy seeds on Saturdays, or, on rainy days, cafés that served thick hot chocolate with whipped cream. We listened to music—Ferenc loved jazz.

By January, the Velvet Revolution had eased much of the cultural and artistic censorship, but Ferenc did not trust the new government's leniency. It was as if he needed the constrictions of communism to define his anger. He was ethnic Hungarian and had a quick temper that made his face red and the veins in his temple throb.

"We are treated like sheep, act like sheep, are sheep."

He took me to amateur plays that took place in artists' garrets or in private apartments. Sometimes there were only ten or so of us sitting on the floor of a three-room apartment—no one had many chairs in those days—while three or four actors presented the plays in a double doorway to a hall. The plays were scenes of authoritarians berating students for writing poems about the French student uprising or for writing about life behind the Wall in East Berlin. Some of the plays were about love affairs of the sort where a girl fell in love with a functionary and then found out he had arrested her uncle for hanging "provocative" paintings in his gallery. The themes reiterated how the Czechs had been continually forced to lie to themselves, how this crisis in their identity undermined creativity and was not something they'd overcome easily, how Communist systems were failing but had left an indelible stain.

During the year that Ferenc and I spent time together, polite as he was, he never made any overtures toward me, never greeted me with a kiss on my cheek or held my arm crossing the street. He spoke fondly about his mother and mentioned he was estranged from his elderly father. His bitterness at having spent a lifetime steeped in socialist values seemed rooted in something deeper than political disgust. I noticed the care he took in his appearance—the way he looped his scarf, wore his jacket over his shoulders like a cape sometimes, kept his old shoes shined, combed his hair back; he had an elegance most men I knew did not have. One night when we were at a concert, a male friend of his came up to us. Ferenc's face lit up as his friend commented about the pianist. I could feel the electricity between them, their private warmth, their private world.

I took note that Ferenc did not introduce me; even so, I could see that my relationship with Ferenc was something special to him. Yet, in spite of his curiosity and intellect, I realized that I'd never spoken easily with him. Fear and shyness, as hard as iron, had barred most of my ideas and feelings despite my need to share them with a man. When I tried to express myself, I became quiet; I couldn't figure out how to get the words that came out of my mouth to mirror the articulate way they formed in my mind. For the first time in my life, I began to try to write out those impressions, but when I did, the same thing happened; the fluid thoughts and sentences became hard and dull on the page. Then it occurred to me that I might address those thoughts to someone. I tried thinking of Ferenc as the target of my imagination, then thought of Katarina. She was the person I was closest to. So I wrote "Dear Katarina" at the top of the pages of what started as laments, but soon become descriptions of things I saw and felt. Feelings, images, memories began to flow onto the paper, page after page, booklet after booklet. I never looked back at them, never reread them—was terrified to. After six months of this, I finally admitted to myself that it wasn't Katarina who had been the target of all of those musings, it was Tomas.

And what did I know? Was our relationship a figment in my mind? What was it from our conversations about translating, from cooking with him at the lake, from a few kisses and hugs, from working with him at his samizdat that stirred such passion in me? Was I just his sister's friend?

Ferenc and I continued to have dinner or go to a play once or twice a month. We laughed that we were like an odd, old couple, reading books in the park, strolling on Sundays. The rest of the time I bent my head to my work, which was becoming more interesting, since I was now allowed to translate from German the stories of Herta Müller and Christa Wolf.

It had been too long since I'd been to see Katarina. She hugged me now only with one limp arm. There were bags under her eyes and a strange defensive laugh that was a shock to see in someone who was always full of affection and energy. Lukas picked fights with Nataša, pulled her doll's head off and threw it across the room. Nataša scribbled pictures of rainbows and stick figures. Georg had joined a soccer team and came home late. When he arrived, he tiptoed past the living room, where I was trying to sleep, to get to the kitchen. The icebox was opened, bottles clanked, the door slammed shut. Katarina waited. Katarina told him to be quiet. Georg yelled at her to be quiet. She yelled back. Their voices grew louder until they tired and both became quiet.

In the mornings Katarina didn't bother to comb her hair. She stirred her tea until it was cold.

"What's wrong? Let's take a walk."

Katarina consented. We walked to the park with the children. I pushed first one then the other on swings. Nataša, looking at older girls swinging high, pumped her legs but could not make the swing climb.

"Push me, Mama," she said, thinking perhaps that Katarina had the right touch, but Katarina was leaning against the fence. She did not hear her daughter's plea.

"Are you okay?" I asked again.

"It's hard. Being a good wife, that is. It sounds strange but I'm lonely with Georg around."

In the apartment, I organized shoes in the hall, lined up Lukas's cars and trucks, dressed Nataša's dolls. I felt helpless. After four days of being with Katarina, I said that I had forgotten a meeting I needed to attend and had to leave early. After that I wrote her at Christmas, sent a doll and a toy dump truck to the children on their birthdays. Katarina didn't respond right away as usual, and the times when I did call her, she sounded distracted.

Uršula and I spoke on the telephone less and less. I was so busy with translations of a collection of essays that I hardly thought to call her. I wished Jakub had come back and had taken her to the Baltic Sea. But Uršula would never have left her house, her chair, her stove, the empty jam jars that needed filling. When I visited her, I was surprised at how she had aged; she was missing a molar, had bad breath, her blouses were not ironed. She limped, her cheeks hung, she puffed going up the stairs. The village, our yard, even the scrawny chickens seemed depleted. Nothing had improved.

Nothing would change. A shutter hung, a door was stuck, dirt in the yard whipped around on windy days, a plastic wrapper was caught on a branch in the plum tree.

One morning in my little apartment, the telephone rang. It was Katarina in tears. She wasn't able to tell me much; Georg was in some kind of trouble and had fallen into a group that was being followed.

"He comes home upset," she said. "He screams at me and at the children. Sometimes he swears so much that I take the children to stay with my friend Irina downstairs." I tried to calm her, said I'd come for a visit the next weekend. She sighed, then changed her tone, became relaxed, and said that all was really not so bad after all, that she was just in a mood, and it would be better for me to wait a few weeks until September, when it would be cooler, and maybe we could go to the lake. I pictured the unkempt apartment, crusty dishes in the sink, Lukas's toys strewn everywhere, piles of dirty clothes.

What I did not know until later was that Tomas had been to see her and was trying to convince her to leave Georg. She had refused, had assured Tomas that Georg was a good father, that it would be unfair to the children, that she was not going to let another divorce in their family leave children embittered. And what would she do all alone at the lake house, the only place that she could afford?

In the middle of a hot summer night, the phone rang. It was Tomas. It had been a few months since we'd had one of our conversations about his job, Katarina, his grandmother's death, or politics. Whatever dream I was having must have been about him; hearing his voice was not surprising, the way it might have been had I been fully awake. His voice was urgent, hard to follow. Something had happened. He was not sure what. Katarina's neighbors had called. Katarina and Georg had not returned from their night out as planned. Tomas was about to drive to their apartment in Brno and asked me to meet him there.

I got out of bed and started packing. I never took much when visiting Katarina, as there was little room there for my things. I pulled out my old cloth suitcase, the one Uršula had bought for me years ago, but it would not shut. I found a bag and began to stuff it with shirts, sweaters, shoes, and then stopped to wonder at my choices. Why heels? Why a jacket when it was mid-August? I went to the kitchen to put on water for tea and forgot what I was looking for in the cupboard. Then it occurred to me to call Katarina, maybe they were back by now. I marveled at my stupidity for not thinking of that before. Dialing, I confused the digits and heard a busy signal. Finally, the call went through. Someone picked up on the other end and then hung up. I arrived at the station an hour early and sat on a wooden bench outside until the doors of the waiting room opened. My hand twitched as I fanned my face. I remembered that I knew nothing, was shaking without reason. I thought of the desperate tone in Tomas's voice.

The door of Katarina's apartment was ajar; it appeared no one was there. Then I heard voices. Tomas talking to people in the living room. I knocked and waited, and when no one came, I stepped in and called Tomas's name. When he came into the hall, I saw it all, more than I feared—it was embedded in his face, in his eyes that looked right into mine. He took me by the elbow and steered me gently into the kitchen.

"Katarina?" was all I could say. He looked at me for a moment, then dropped his head and covered his eyes with his left hand.

"It was their neighbor Irina who called," he finally said. "They had been at a celebration for a soccer tournament. Irina became alarmed that something had happened because Katarina told her that they'd be back early, around nine. An hour ago his car was found south of the city, crashed into a tree."

My mouth went dry. That was what I noticed first, being parched. Then I saw the kitchen: it was clean, everything had been put away, the soap was tilted on its side, a few bubbles had dried on the rim of the sink. Outside, a police car was parked across the street, a woman was walking her dog, the sky was cloudy, leaves rustled in a tree. Tomas and I stood, unable to speak, to move, me with my hand steadying myself on the counter, he next to me, our shoulders touching. A dog barked. I heard the sound of pigeons rising up from the sidewalk, their wings fluttering, dozens of them in the air, arching, flying, dipping until that was all I saw, a flock of gray and white birds chased from breadcrumbs, hovering in the morning air. And then the sun peeked out from behind a cloud, spilling onto the counter, spreading its light across the room, illuminating the kettle on the stove, the empty milk bottles, the handle on the door.

URŠULA

Pavlas Cottage
Bohemia

Zofie. It is a year. You are in Prague. You will come back here, but not forever. My handwriting is not readable, the alphabet letters jag. But now I am hearing some strange messages, they are trapped in my head, so I need to talk, but I can't, you are not here, you cannot hear me. The words would not come out anyway.

Today there is sun. There is always sun in my mind. Sun above clouds. Sun behind the night. Sun around the hill before it blazes through trees. My mother and brother were the sun, but their memory did not always rise. I could not see them, because they were in fog. I could not think of them until a few weeks ago.

Sometimes, while opening a jar, there's my mother's hand on the lid. I see her skin spots, her blue veins twisting the top until it pops when it comes off. There is the clack clack of Milan's soccer ball kicking against the shed. Every afternoon, kicking the ball even when there was no longer air in it. There is my father's voice, hard, angry, bouncing off the kitchen walls. Those are sounds. They do not need sun to hear.

I'm on the front step, remembering. I had a red-checked dishcloth doll. Nina didn't have a face but I fed her a pretend bottle. I'd sit on the front step, put her on my shoulder, pat her back. My mother would say, "How's your doll today?" Nina couldn't talk. I heard her thinking. I could not tell my mother what she was feeling. I didn't talk either. Not until I was eight.

"Talk!" my father yelled at me. "Everyone must. It is life to talk." At dinner he'd say, "What did you learn in kindergarten? What did you have for lunch? Did you rake the leaves?" But no words came out. I heard them behind my face, but they were stuck. My father's fist landed hard on the table. Plates rose up and clattered down, I dropped my head, my face reddened, my wooden shoes fell off my feet onto the floor.

Now I'm in the parlor. There is a high shelf. The chairs are whittled from pine trees. Four face the stove. A window looks west. Nina, my doll, lived on a shelf above that window. She starved. She cried. She slept. She cried. She watched me. She hated me. I could not reach her. Not even with two chairs stacked and falling. Nina was as angry as my father. "You cannot have her," he'd say, "until you talk."

"I'll have tea now," my father would say. My mother made tea. "Make room for wood." I cleaned ashes out of the stove. "Take care of Milan." My mother worked at the cannery. My father at the bullet factory. I took care of my younger brother. "Take care of Milan," my father would say evenings he played cards at the bullet factory cafeteria.

It is another day. I'm remembering again. It is the way it was a long time ago. Looking out the parlor window, I'd spin: red curtains, yellow picture frame, wood rafters in the low ceiling, the carved date on the door, the trees and road and the hill through the thick panes go in and out of focus like a kaleidoscope. I waited afternoons in October for the chug of the Magyar Circus trucks on the dirt road. How could I make the circus come sooner? But the circus came after leaves had blown. The five canvas-covered trucks clanked. The drivers ground gears to go uphill. I followed. They parked in a circle. Men women children jumped onto burned-out grass. They rolled up canvas sides. A round-rumped brown horse clopped down a ramp. Trick dogs followed, lifting legs on the tires, then running in the field. Dust settled. Men unloaded tents, poles, ropes, trapeze bars, wooden rails. I watched as they built the ring.

I did not tell you about the circus. I did not think about it all those years. The circus died, and other death memories were hidden in that fog. After the last circus came, Nazis made us so hungry that we ate wilted cabbage, soggy beets, and sprouted onions. We waited in lines for bread. We marched, sang Nazi national songs. Our right arms flew in the air to salute. Wilpstien the cobbler, Gippen the tailor sewed yellow stars on their sleeves. They went to the station. We never saw them again. That winter, eggs were saved for soldiers. Flour was poured into paper sacks to ration. Farmers cheese was potted in glass jars. It was picked up on Mondays. Two women with short bangs in uniforms drove a small round car. Our plums were pruned for soldiers. The house became quiet after my father was sent to Poland. Workhorses in the village were driven in a herd of dust down the road.

The brown circus horse was gone too. He with his trusting eyes. He who now had to pull overloaded munitions wagons or was ground up for meat. It was the end of his act. The end of his long-flowing mane. The end of his long-flowing tail as he cantered with his rider wearing a white peasant's blouse, with his rider's sleeves flapping. The rider flipping forward, then balancing on the horse's back, then jumping through a hoop flaming with fire.

Three years there was the circus. At the last, my father held Milan's hand after he bought the tickets. My mother stood a long time and looked at flapping colors of the Hungarian and Romanian flags. We sat on bleachers. Two men, in red coats and white breeches, drummed. Girls in blue stockings, in blue bathing suits with arched backs, flew from swing to swing. Mutts, in studded collars, sailed over hurdles. Men juggled, their wooden pins criss-crossed. A woman bent herself in half, and twisted her legs over her shoulders. The clown's pants fell off when he somersaulted.

And then a dwarf with a wrinkled face and melon-colored hair and a glass crown and a pink swishing hoop skirt walked around the audience. She was looking for one person. Up and down the bleachers she went, her skirt swaying, her hand over her eyes as she looked to the left and the right. She looked at girls from the village, she cooed at a baby, she winked at Milan, she stopped in front of me.

"What is your name?" she asked. Her voice was friendly.

"Uršula," I answered out loud.

"How old are you?" she asked.

"Eight," I said.

"Here's a present," she said. She gave me a cloth bag. "You are the special person today." She patted my cheek. She smiled. She picked up the side of her skirt, walked down the seats, and disappeared behind the curtain. I squeezed the little bag and felt six round shapes. I untied the ribbon and opened the bag and smelled cinnamon candy.

After that words came out. Never many. So Nina was given back. I looked at her, she was not inside of herself. I could not hear her think. I held her the way I used to, but she was just a faded dishtowel tied around a walnut head. I had loved her. Now I felt nothing. I was not even sad. I wanted to love her. I wanted to pat her back and rock her. But she was gone. Later, when Nina fell behind my bed, I didn't notice. I found her wedged: her dress gnawed by moths or mice, her walnut head pulpy.

There was nothing left to love. Everything changed. Tuberculosis took first my brother, Milan. My parents coughed. I held cloths to their mouths. They rasped. I fed them spoonful after spoonful of soup. I put cloths on their foreheads until they were gone and I had to tell the undertaker there were no more breaths.

But Zofie how you could speak. You were making up sounds as I used to do for Nina. Words and words came out of you when you were two. When boarders came you asked, "What's in your suitcase, what color are your tongues, do you want me to bring your slippers, why are you leaving so soon?"

When you were four, a young East German couple stayed for the month of July. They came to walk on roads and through villages. Their grandparents were Bohemian. They wanted to find their roots. They taught you songs. You sang with them in German. Gerhardt whistled tunes in the orchard. You followed. You did not talk for a few days after they left. I never mentioned them again.

Sometimes you became very silent. You observed the boarders, furrowing your brow, staring, shaking your head. What were you learning? You paid attention. You asked questions. Were you hoping to find your parents? Did you then notice how old I was? How stiff? And that I did not clap for you or say how smart you were, that you could talk as easily as a flowing river?

Another message. I feel it in my head. I'm in front of the mirror in my room. It is an oval oak mirror with side hinges. It swivels up or down. It is facing down. It is looking at the rug, at the knots and loops and colors in that old rug my mother made. It is made from ripped-up strips of shirts and pants and skirts. Milan's and my childhood are in our torn clothes. My mother braided and braided. She looped and sewed the cloth braids into a circle. Every winter more was added. It's by the window now and I can see my blue smock and my red and white kindergarten pinafore and Milan's brown shorts he wore to school and the collar of my first white blouse and knee socks and Milan's blue socks my mother knitted and darned. The border is my green sweater with buttons on the neck. There is my red corduroy skirt. Now, barefoot, I am stepping on Milan and me.

I turn the mirror toward the window. It can look at the chicken shed, the orchard, the field, or at the sky changing. I am old and know mirrors don't think but I know this mirror does not always want to stare into a room. It does not want to look at the rug. It does not want to stare into the corner where there are hooks, or at the ceiling with cracks and one light bulb on a frayed wire. It does not want to look at me when I am sleeping.

Now the mirror is tilted to look at me. I forget I am me. I work and work. Cooking and scrubbing. Collecting eggs and stirring stew. I forget I have a body that moves me around my chores.

I forget I wear work shoes and unlace those shoes at night. I forget I brush my hair without looking. And that I am older. And that inside of my face, behind my hazel eyes and cheeks made rough from too much sun, there are these new thoughts. I forget that inside those thoughts there are moments, seconds, days of long ago. Now they appear in flashes.

"Uršula," I say to myself, "you do not want closeness." So I do not speak much. No one knows what I am thinking. Words get mixed up. Better to be quiet.

My father said, "A dwarf, a simpleton, a circus misfit made you finally talk."

I am not beautiful. I am not sure but I know. I lug my feet upstairs. My upper arms sway when I clip clothes on the line. My hair is gray. It is falling out. Buttons of my blouse burst from buttonholes. My slip I see in the reflection of the mirror is lower than my skirt. My cheeks are heavy, they have drooped. I know I am not beautiful. I don't know conversations. No one talks to me. I don't talk about the nature I see. I don't talk about winter frost on bushes at the stream.

I never thought about me until Jakub noticed a long time ago. Then I looked in the mirror. What was he seeing? I was not swollen back then. My hair was brown. He gave me a stick of lipstick. I put it on. Something happened in the mirror. From plain, I saw pretty.

Here is another message. It is pressing my ears. You had a story. Why had you been left? Where did you come from? Was it the dwarf lady? My wish for another Nina? A wish I did not say out loud. But the dwarf lady was by then dead. Sometimes you scared me. You peered into yourself. You peered beyond yourself. Beyond a reflection in a mirror. Your quiet was mysterious. I could not know your world. My knowing stopped when Nina was put on the shelf.

I wondered. Were you from a city? Were you from a faraway country? Were you a princess? You walked in fields at sunset or in the woods. What did you think about? You filled the bird feeder and talked to the sparrows. You did homework. You were bent over pages I did not understand. You learned words in other languages. You had moods. I was not allowed. You sat at the kitchen table and made profiles of faces and floor plans of houses with rooms for sisters and brothers and mothers and fathers.

Another message. At your first cry I did not want you. In a hurry to get laundry from the rain, I left you on the hearth.

After, I softened. I would care for you. For a day, a week, forever. You slept in a drawer in my room. Bundled in the blanket you had arrived in, you watched while I made beds for boarders and cooked. I carried you from room to room in a straw basket. In a year, you began to speak. Sentences flowed. Your eyes widened as you looked around. Was I good enough?

I see parts of the world in people. In the pleats of pants I iron. A comrade says something, another responds. City people come. People come from faraway places. From trains into Prague and other Iron Curtain countries. Jakub invited me to the Baltic. "To see seagulls, villages, beach and waves," he said. Apparatchiks talk about agriculture. Franta always held a book under his arm. He went to the garden bench to read. He gave you books. He knew you deserved more.

I think about the dwarf lady. At night I stare up at the cracks in the ceiling. I go back to childhood moments. The swish of the dwarf lady's puffy skirt on the bleachers of the circus tent. She walks closer to me. There is a glow around her hair. She pats my cheeks. Her fingers are warm. My face flushes. Her eyes are as blue as cornflowers. She smiles and gives me herself.

In a dream I have many times, the dwarf lady is lying under a tree in dappled shade. It is hot. Her arms open like an angel.

Her pink skirt collapses onto her legs. She peers up into the tree. Light sparkles on her. A breeze cools her.

My mother said, "The lady at the circus was a magician. She chose you, Uršula. She touched you. You, too, will touch someone."

Would I become a dwarf? I looked in the mirror. Was I a dwarf? The circus lady had broken my silence. I never ate the candy. I was scared of it. Eating it could make words go away. The bag got dusty. The seams came undone. The bag fell apart on the shelf. The scent was gone.

Even when words came, I could not make myself right. Smiles are stuck behind my face. I could not touch you or hug you. Would I hit you? For not talking right. For saying something wrong, like my father did to me. After my parents died, I would always live in this cottage. All who came—the boarders, the East German couple, Jakub, you—would leave.

One person stayed on in the village. He too would never leave. He was born here. He is Eva's father, Vilem. I needed help with the shed. He seemed to know and stopped by two weeks ago. I was tired of hearing the boarders make noises. They stay up late. Vilem returned with a workman and tools. They hammered and plastered a room for me. They installed a water closet. He and I painted the room yellow with leftover paint that Vilem and Viktorie had used to paint Eva's room.

In kindergarten, Vilem and I were in the same class. He saw me coming to school alone. Sometimes he waited. I did not raise my hand in class. I did not speak. During recess we played "family." He was the father. He chopped wood with a stick. I was the mother. I cooked with pretend pots. I stirred with my hand. Or I was the grandmother and he was the grandchild. He had to herd our sheep. Or we were sister and brother horses that ran off into the fields. He assigned our roles. He showed me how to move, how to stir, when to be a horse and follow him at a canter.

When we were sixteen, or was it fifteen, our paths crossed once in the woods. It was evening. Vilem was walking, I could hear him coming. I could hear folk songs on the transistor radio he always carried. When he saw me he said, "Let's collect things for a mobile." What was a mobile? He had string in his pocket. He had feathers and a dead butterfly. He hung a branch from the birch tree by the brook. We found feathers, stones, bones, bent-shaped twigs, and a snakeskin. In time, together, alone, we added, repaired, and adjusted it. Once, weeks later, we sat on a log and watched the floating objects waver or collide or twirl. We made layers of twigs hanging from yarn with quartz pebbles, fragments of tortoise shells, wasp nests, and broken birds' eggs. They balanced from willow branches. When I go back to the brook, I look up to see what remains. Only Vilem and I would recognize the frayed string, the dangling twigs, a walnut shell, and a lone wishbone I added many years ago that is still there.

Viktorie came to work as a seamstress. She's younger. How she laughed. How she and Vilem laughed. In the market, in the café, seated side by side on the steps at the village fountain. Sometimes when I passed, Vilem patted the bench for me to join. But I cannot laugh.

When we finished the room, Vilem put his paintbrush into the pail and said, "It's not the same without Zofie." All at once, as if rays of sun poured light into my head, I guessed how you came into my life. Vilem had dropped you off. To give me a "family" like we had when we played. We were a mother and a daughter.

I asked him. "Is that how she came?" Vilem raised his eyebrows. He said he had never told anyone. Not even Viktorie. "But where did the baby come from?" "My cousin Emilia," he explained. Emilia had arrived in a car with young people. It was after the two hundred thousand Soviet troops invaded

Prague. News had crackled onto the transistor radio. Tanks from East Germany and Poland and Hungary and Bulgaria rolled through the countryside at night. Then, two days later, as rain and fog and wind blew in the yard in the village, Vilem heard knocking on the door and opened it to find Emilia.

Emilia was a nurse who lived outside of Prague. That morning she had bags under her eyes, her hair was uncombed, and there was a sleeping baby in her arms. "I need to borrow money. We have to leave right away. Soviets are heading to the borders. We could be arrested. Friends have been caught." A man in the car told her to hurry up. "We can't take this baby," Emilia told Vilem. "She's not mine. The phone lines are off. I can't reach her mother. Please take the child. Her mother will come soon." "It was a risk," Vilem told me, but he did not think that the misplaced mother would show up in our village. He never heard from Emilia again.

Now it is evening. The air is calm, it is quiet here at our cottage. I am tired of the remembering for now. I think I'll lie under a tree with my arms stretched out by my side. I'll close my eyes and feel the last of the sun through the leaves. As you know, the largest plum tree in the orchard has arching limbs, and underneath, the ground is soft, the grass long.

MARIA

Stone House
Angelsey, Wales

It is snowing here, snowing hard now, blanketing the horses in the field, icing the fruit trees, covering the stone wall, falling into the Atlantic, sheets of white into gray water. I am facing west. I placed my desk here so I can stare at the water for hours, into that void where my thoughts become calm, where, if I focus on sounds of the radiator, the dog twitching, a tractor in the alley, my mind releases the need for sighs, for regret. And still, after all of these years, Zofie, I can't accept what happened, am not in control of emotions. It is right, it is sad. Right as it is natural for a mother to mourn the loss of her child, but you are still alive. You *must* be alive. It is useless to dwell on what I seem not to be able to know—where you are—as that unknowing gnaws at me, eats away at the care and love Edward gives, and at the love I feel for Teddy. Teddy is adorable, and now, at age nine, with freckles and a dimple on his chin, and lean like his father, he asks questions. Where were you born, Mum? Who was your mother? Why was your father always old? When I begin to tell him, he wants more. Why don't we go to Prague? Where is Prague? Why is it not here in Wales?

Everything now is new—Edward, Teddy, a stone house looking into the ocean. This country and the language I speak that Teddy tells me sounds wooden in my mouth. Teddy with his nutty-smelling hair and a tooth chipped from a fall; his adventures in the woods with his sack on a stick; his head on my chest after dinner, sleeping, my arms around his waist, while Edward and I linger at the table, talking.

"Can we go now?" Teddy demands as soon as Edward comes home from teaching. Every day they go outside to play, to work. Until Teddy was four, Edward would carry him on his shoulders to the shore. They'd stand for a while watching the waves. I could see them from the house. A totem pole of two. "Will the waves rise? Will they crash into the house?" Edward told me Teddy always asked.

Now it is April and I see Teddy and Edward working on the stone wall. We have a view of the sea that we said we wanted when we looked for a house. It is the view I needed toward the west. I think Edward does not notice that I orient myself looking away from the east; in restaurants, in conversations, in my darkroom, in moments where I can choose, I stand or sit with my back to the past.

Teddy is walking along the finished part of the wall with his arms out, as if on a tightrope. Edward has pulled stones off from where he had placed them last week and is standing up now. I notice he's wearing the turtle-size kneepads—a gift from Mr. Craw, a farmer down the road—and I think that his back must be sore, because his hands are massaging his hips. He had originally consulted with Mr. Craw, who took him around the county to show him different kinds of walls. Edward's wall appears to be a mixture of anything possible to keep it from crumbling, and is more like a serpentine sculpture than a wall that might contain livestock.

As I watch them, I cannot help but think of you. It is your birthday today. You are fourteen. I was fourteen when my mother died. I used to write you letters, but as I had no address to send them to, I threw them away as I wrote them. I guess I felt words could not repair our separation. I wake up on this day every year and remember details of your birth, the feelings I never expected, never hoped for, nor would have thought about at age nineteen. During your birth I felt that I, too, was being born as you made your way into the world, coming from such a hidden place into my arms. Torn from roots was how it felt. Roots now hidden, roots you must want to understand. You, whom I can now only try to imagine.

I have decided to write down some paragraphs of my memories, which come and go in spurts and starts. I hope one day I can show you this notebook about my childhood and my family. This is what I can give you now. I still imagine that one day I will be able to share with you my life so you can make sense of yours.

* * *

Prague:

It had snowed all night and all day and through the next night. The tram could no longer run up to our Dejvice neighborhood. The streets were quiet; my father stayed in his garret studio rather than trek through the snow to the museum. My mother and I shoveled paths through the backyard for Zola, our dog. Ema, my grandmother, stood at the stove, scooping dumplings from boiling water; steam clouded the windows. Debussy on Ema's radio crackled with static. Though it was late February, it felt like Christmas. There was no school. Coal smoke from our neighbors' chimneys rose into the blizzard. Our coats hung on hooks by the front door; our hats and mittens lay on the floor, crusted and stiff with slowly melting ice. Then, as if a curtain were opening, the storm faded away and the sun came out, briefly warming the air before the cold night arrived.

"Look!" my mother said the next morning at breakfast. "Look at the chairs on the terrace!" She stood to reach for her camera, her mouth forming into a smile of expectation and excitement. "Let's go!" We pulled on our boots and hats, buttoned up wool coats; she looped her light meter around her neck and the Leica over her shoulder. Yesterday's afternoon sun had warmed the iron chairs enough so that the eight-inch snow pillows covering the seats had begun to slide before the cold night air froze them into place, like tilted top hats. Later, in the darkroom, as we watched the first black of the backs of the iron chairs emerge through the Dektol, and then the gray of winter branches in the background and the sugar white of snow pillows appear, my mother, lifting one side of the developing pan and then the other to move the chemicals evenly over the paper, said, "The exposure is perfect. This one we'll keep."

*　*　*

Wednesdays, the elementary school I attended in Prague ended at noon. Every so often my mother would surprise me. She'd be standing alongside her Skoda, smoking a cigarette, with her wavy auburn hair pulled back into a loose bun, her long sweater unbuttoned, one of her mischievous smiles sneaking across her face. I would be saved the tram ride home. I'd not spend the afternoon with Loti, my neighbor, or walk my dog Zola around the block, or do homework with Ema interrupting me, eager to quiz me. "Let's have a picnic," my mother might say, or "Let's visit your father at the museum," or "How about a walk in the park?" She always appeared animated when she saw me, even after just a morning of separation. We would have a picnic; we'd drive to the river or a park, spread out the blanket she kept in the car, and unpack a basket Ema had prepared of salami, wrapped hot hard-boiled eggs, apple juice, and apple cake. We would lie back and look at the leaves above us, or clouds, and talk about friends or people she photographed. But this was only after she had set up her camera on a tripod aimed at a reflection of trees in a pond or at orchards on the Strahov hill across the river. She was prepared for the light to grow intense; she was patient. She liked sharing afternoons when she could escape from the studio she worked in. She needed the satisfaction of making new photographs.

One day we surprised my father at his laboratory at the National Gallery. After climbing the winding stone stairway to his office and being told he was in a meeting, we went back outside, as it was a beautiful fall day. We settled onto the steps, my mother's elbow propped, her other hand waved around as she spoke, when she suddenly sat up and said, "Maria, look at that chestnut cart. That's the same one that was here the afternoon I met your father."

I was told it happened on a day that my father, Johan, had been scraping paint, a day of mixing colors, making tests on gessoed canvas, clearing ancient oils with thinner. The muslin curtains were closed, the sun impeded from seeping in. My father worked under a dim yellow bulb so the pigments were represented as if in the glow of candlelight. The painting, Flemish, by a minor painter, given to the museum in the '30s, had been hidden by my father from the Nazis in the '40s. Now, in 1946, he had time to clean it. My father said that in the back of his mind, somewhere behind the headache that throbbed from squinting, from the hunger he became aware of when his stomach growled, he remembered the exhibition opening that would take place that evening in the main gallery of the museum.

He had been going to every opening he could, ironing his one white shirt, brushing lint from his one suit, shining his shoes so that he would not stand out, not appear to look like a museum employee who worked in restoration. Though he was the observer, the young man who slipped into studio openings uninvited, the young man in homespun wool who took notes as he looked at every painting or exhibition of drawings, he was never questioned, never asked to leave, but he rarely stayed long. Sometimes the patrons would greet him, sometimes a person standing next to him while look-ing at a painting would talk to him, but my father, aware of the lenience and elegance of the cultured class who were able to maintain that elegance in spite of the somber veil of Communist repression, nodded politely or merely expressed appreciation for the art.

He later told me his version: How the afternoon glare from the setting sun bothered him, as he walked outside for some air before he'd make his way through the long halls of the museum to the gallery. As the head of restoration of medieval art in this museum, he was expected at this opening and would feel comfortable sipping Sekt, but now he needed to put something into his stomach. Chestnuts, warm chestnuts, were what he had thought about when he descended into the plaza in front of the museum—a cone of newspaper folded around chestnuts that had been roasted, now with their shells cracked, the heat of the bundle softening tendons in his hand, stiff from meticulous work. The cart was there, at the bottom of the steps near the street, and the chestnut seller was poking at the coals under the griddle while listening to a young woman—a woman my father had seen and admired from a distance. He'd even dreamed about her a few nights before, a dream he could not recall other than that in it he seemed to have been in conversation with her. Over the last few years, he had noticed her at most of the studio openings. Now here she was, at ease chatting, as he had often seen her, her hair long down her back, a dark-blue cape fastened around her neck with a red-cloth frog button, flat shoes, and stockings—even with the shortage of silk in stores. Freckles on her cheeks gave her a healthy glow in winter. He told me that he waited on the steps until she had paid, and then he watched her step away, her cape fluttering in the breeze. He was sure she'd walk off or up to the museum entrance.

But she turned, raised her eyebrows at my father, and said, "These are the best chestnuts, don't you think?"

It was a cool evening, the sun was low. My father led the way to the gallery. Their footsteps—his in old black shoes, hers in suede—were in stride walking down the long parquet floor. Italian paintings on loan from a Dresden museum did not please the woman named Lydie. "Too complex," she said. "Too many religious stories. I prefer the hinter-ground horizons, the Byzantine blue in the sky, and hills, and panoramas."

* * *

Friday nights my father and mother and I went to informal art openings. My father loved to bargain and was often able to buy a sketch or a painting or maybe an etching from a previous exhibition. Many of those evenings took place in the artists' studios. Holding my parents' hands as we walked though a dark courtyard, I was scared but not scared. Branches hung over iron fences like arms trying to get us. My father hummed, and the glow of my mother's cigarette and the smell of smoke were comforting. We saw the light of a window and heard voices, and soon we saw people standing outside smoking, or they were in the doorway waiting to squeeze into the small space. My parents greeted friends with handshakes, and those friends bent down to greet me, shaking my hand or patting me on my back as we worked our way inside. Music played on a radio station or sometimes on a gramophone; there was the hum of people talking. We did not stay long, but I liked the chatter, it sounded like birds in trees. I listened to the sounds of laughter, and noticed the aroma of the plum liquor people were drinking out of small glasses. The lights were turned to shine on the wall of drawings, but it bounced from the walls and broke apart into shadows. My father held my hand, leading me to the table to get his plum drink, leading me to look at the art, explaining how this artist used charcoal, that even though the image appeared only black and white, the artist had used many shades of blacks and grays. It was often stuffy in the studios, usually one of the doors was left open. There was always the sound of the people who were still outside. After we left, my father took me to a window, lifted me up so I could see into the room, and said that I should think of the room as a painting. Everything appeared farther away, the light was soft, the people were lingering in groups. Everything blended into what my father called composition.

My mother not only made but collected photographs. Sometimes I went with her to the State-run studio, Fotografia, in the afternoons, when four or five of the photographers who used the space met to talk about their work and trade photographs. The conversation was technical. There were concerns about getting chemicals. They gave each other advice about printing. They talked about how long an East German developer could last compared to the Hungarian brand. The smell of Dektol and Dimezone and what they call fixer was strong—stronger than it was in the basement closet my mother used as a dark room. I got headaches and became quickly bored and couldn't wait to be back in her car going home. Often, under her arm was a box with one or two new images that she was going to add to her favorites and that my father, when he went to see his mother, Babicka, took with him to store in her attic.

*   *   *

Our stucco Dejvice villa was passed down from Ema's father to her and Opa. They had moved out to let my parents and me live there and then Ema moved back in after Opa died. The rooms, though chilly, seemed warm to me, with lamps lit for reading or candles burning on nights when the city had blackouts from power failures. Evenings, Ema and my mother read books to me, and my father told stories about the paintings in the museum. We spent winter afternoons comparing or considering watercolor compositions and artistic styles. On Sundays we looked up German and Hungarian and Italian cities in the encyclopedia, read about Gothic and Romanesque architecture, drew maps of streets, made up stories about trips there: the bridges we'd cross in Budapest, and which church we'd visit in Dresden, boat rides on the Danube.

As a photographer, my mother looked for light. As an art restorer, my father restored light. Prague in those years, in spite of the faded colors of the elaborate façades of the Baroque buildings, seemed like a sad city. Cloud cover from winter inversions clung to the castle hill and over the river for months. At times one could not see from one end of an avenue to the next. In the suburbs, Soviet-run factories making armaments and cheap clothing and poorly made toasters or ovens or heaters churned out black soot from tall brick stacks. Smells of chemicals floated in the air. As snow turned to slush, puddles flooded doorways. Gutters were clogged. Garbage was not picked up, and rain seemed to fall for weeks. My mother retreated to the darkroom. My father spent weekends hidden in his studio.

But spring was spring. Sun peeped through clouds and warmed my mother as she'd lie on a chair in the garden, hoping to tan her face; or on Ema's shoulders as she hung clothes on the line; or it warmed us all at a park, having a picnic. "There is always something worthwhile to appreciate," my mother often remarked as we set off to the grocery store or to buy a special photographic paper. She'd stop on one of the bridges and point out the different kinds of fishing boats waiting to get through the locks. If we saw a family dressed in tattered clothes she'd make up a story about how they were singers and had come to the city to find work.

*   *   *

One afternoon when I was fourteen, Ema and I happened to be on the same Hanspauka-bound trolley. We walked up the street from the stop, she swinging her purse with each step. Her lipstick was freshly applied, her hair blew about in the breeze. My school pack was heavy. I thought it was no longer right to wear it on my back, so I was clutching it in front of me. It was full of books for homework and library books for the weekend. When we turned into our street, I noticed that the sun was behind a cloud, that fall was ending. "It's chilly," Ema remarked. "An afternoon for reading and knitting."

We heard moaning the moment we were inside the house, and then we saw my mother on the couch, curled up, her hair messy, fallen from its bun, strands sticking to sweat on her forehead. Zola was at her feet, whimpering. "Call for help," my mother said, "No, go for help. I'm splitting inside." There was no one on the street when I ran outside, and Loti's villa was dark. Zola barked at the door when I left her. The Skoda was parked in the back alley. I rushed from the yard into the house and told Ema we had to drive. I knew my mother couldn't, and Ema had never learned, so it was up to me. Ema said no, we might crash, but my mother, desperate, stood up, bent in half, and shuffled to the door, leaning on the handle to catch her breath, moaning as she went down the steps. She curled into the back seat. Ema shook her head. I found the keys on the floor and told Ema to get in. I managed to get the car turned on, my foot let out the clutch, and the car moved into the street. I shut down my mind—my fear—and focused on the few times last summer when my mother and I were in the countryside on dirt roads and, after we had finished photographing for the day, my mother had stopped the car and said, "Your turn. Your grandfather taught me when I was your age. It's about timing: clutch in, shift the gear, clutch out, accelerate." The car had lurched the first, the second time, even the third time, but I soon understood. I drove down hills, around curves, out of a valley, along fields shorn of corn. Zola stood on the door handle, her nose out the window, ears flying.

We did not make it to the hospital in time for a successful operation. Infection had already spread through her body. As you can imagine, my mother's ruptured appendix tore the light out of our lives.

*   *   *

I was at breakfast one morning the summer after my mother died. The window was open, birds pecked at seeds in Ema's feeder. It was a day I might look for Loti, a day we'd walk to the teahouse in the park to meet friends for cake. I was washing yogurt from porcelain bowls, not thinking, when I turned off the faucet, walked to the cellar door, opened it, walked down the steps I'd not walked down in months. I opened the darkroom door. I'd had dreams of opening that door, dreams of my mother's ghost—rubber apron and rubber gloves and wooden shoes standing in front of the sink of trays, wooden prongs held in the right glove, moving a wet photograph into the fixer. I switched on the light. The room was as she left it, she was not there in any way. I knew what I was looking for. Her camera. I put it around my neck. I closed the door.

Upstairs, through the viewfinder, there were slants of light coming through the window. Reflected in the mirror, I noticed the pitcher of pansies on the front hall table, and outside the windows, shadows of trees were leaning over iron fences, lying as if fallen on streets. I focused the lens to see cracks in a teacup, veins in a sliced plum, and tributaries of veins on Ema's hand. I clicked, though there was no film. In one frame, the hairs in Zola's dachshund coat, in others, the leaves wavering on the kitchen wall, white-enamel pots above the stove, wooden spoons.

Ema, reading Chekhov on the couch, jumped in fright, turned to find me behind her, aiming the camera lens onto her halo of white hair lit up by the standing lamp, and said, "Oh, it's you. You're worse than your mother. My hair is my hair. Find something else to scrutinize with your lens."

My father, in his studio, mixing colors from tubes of

paint, put down his easel, noticed me clicking the camera onto the tripod, and said, "This summer you can catalog broken statues at the museum in payment for film."

*   *   *

It is hard to think of the Iron Curtain and the oppression of communism that you must have endured, but it was perhaps not that different than it was for me, though the oppression I've read about now in Czechoslovakia is at times worse than before. I was not able to imagine life to be otherwise until I got used to living in Wales. I was born in 1949, and although I have my fond memories of everyday moments, my parents, in hushed voices, talked about how life had changed: the cold house, coal shortages, cold water, long lines in winter for cheese and meat, my mother hiding her wartime photographs of Jews waiting in lines with suitcases. There was no hope for an end to censorship, schools were controlled by district apparatchiks, petrol was rationed, and what Ema always lamented—the millions of windows in Prague that were no longer washed, that scum collected in the park ponds, and beet and cabbage patches grew in place of roses. She was worried about having a granddaughter growing up in these times, and sad that we couldn't travel. Yet stores were open, though what was displayed and available was controlled. People still came to each other's houses for coffee, children played in the park, people married and had babies. Artists and photographers and poets found ways to express themselves in spite of the system.

*   *   *

I spent three summers after my mother died at Babicka's cottage. I was not happy going there. I had been a few times with my parents, as my father used to love coming back to the farm. We went on walks by the river, collected eggs, fed the cows, and drew pictures of the barn and their straw-thatched house with stubs of crayons Babicka had saved from his childhood. Now, there was nothing to do. Babicka was up at five, shucking walnuts, kneading bread, scuffling about feeding the chickens, spreading corn for them to peck, and sweeping the front yard. I could hear her broom swishing over the dried dirt, back and forth just under my window, which was always open because it was hot. Back and forth her homemade twig broom swept with that swish swish sound, shaming me who was still in bed, who never wanted to get up. I tossed, the mattress creaked. Was it sixteen-year-old restlessness? Was it because I was forced to come to my father's childhood cottage because my father could not have me wandering around the streets all summer looking for my mother in scenes she might have photographed? Was it because Babicka chose to make her own broom and sent me to collect twigs in the forest like a child in a fairy tale? They were to be straight—"Or don't bother to pick them

143

up," she'd tell me—and then she'd measure them, line them up on the edge of the front door step, saw the ends with her crooked little saw, and wrap them around the old birch stick with baling wire, her breath wheezing, wisps of her hair fallen about her face. She admired her handiwork, holding the broom in front of her as if she had made a sculpture.

I guess it was different now that I was older. When I was younger, Babicka could make our games seem real. In our hands, the homemade rag dolls with beautiful painted faces did flips or flew around the room as she made whooshing sounds. Hers was an acrobat, mine a fairy. What freedom they had. How we laughed as they careened around the kitchen table, or flew out the front door before dipping to come back. The fun lasted until she'd announce that her doll was tired or it was time to make dinner. We put them to bed in shoes. And there they remained in a closet—lying face up with their big eyes open—in clogs or slippers until we played with them the next time.

Another time at Babicka's cottage, I had my camera. I always got up late. Babicka had left bread and coffee on the table. There was a pot of her plum jam and a wedge of butter, butter she had churned from cream that Milna, her old cow, had produced. This was where I was happiest at her house— if I had to find one moment those days—sitting alone late mornings at the table in that kitchen redolent of wood smoke, coffee, apples, and yeast. Milna slept out by the back door. At times I heard her snoring, and then she woke up and mooed, her head arched, her tail rose up to ward off flies— back and forth it swiped, like Babicka's broom. Babicka was in the garden as usual, bent over—her skirt hiked up above her knees, the bow of her apron starched—throwing weeds into a pail. Trying to ignore how hard she was working, I scanned the pots, the coats on hooks, something inside to photograph. I noticed a bowl of fruit with two plums and an apricot. The noonday light from the east window fell onto the skin of the plums, but the apricot was shaded in the background. I took my time setting up my tripod to take a long exposure, when I noticed Babicka, who, as she came into the kitchen, stopped and watched as I moved the bowl into the shaft of sun so the skin of the apricot was luminous.

The next morning on the windowsill were two braided bunches of garlics with long stems; brown eggs were arranged on a white platter; the apricot and plums were in a small blue and white bowl. Sprigs of rosemary and oregano had been arranged in an oval shape on a cutting board. "Come here," Babicka said when she saw me noticing. She took my hand and led me on a tour of the yard. "Look at the firewood, and the willows, and the crisscross of the hen-house ladder, and the rows in the vegetable garden. It's about patterns," she said. "Patterns," she repeated, "they are everywhere."

It snowed the day I met your father at the seminar. One of those late winter storms that blew in from the Tatra Mountains. I walked backwards a few steps now and again but then forged forward. I covered my eyes from the stabbing sleet as I crossed the university commons. The lecture hall, though, was warm. I sat in the front row and waited for the young professor, Anton Darovosky, from Odessa, to begin. With his hands on the lectern, he watched as students unwound scarves, slipped from coats, shuffled papers, settled in seats. After introducing himself, he began to read a poem by the famous Czech poet Jaroslav Kvapil. Anton Darovosky's voice was calm and it flowed from stanza to stanza, even with his strong accent. Between stanzas, his dark eyes rose from his notes and scanned the room, as his right hand turned the page. He read the short poem in French, then in German and in Russian and in Czech. No one stirred, no one coughed. He closed the book, marked his place with his forefinger, stepped away from the lectern, walked to the edge of the stage, opened the book, and read the poem again in each of the languages. And then he closed the book and held it behind him. He talked about sounds—the tone of words, melody, and cadence, and how when written in languages not known to those in the audience, a poem had to carry emotion, it should resonate like an aria.

I now recall how during that moment I allowed myself

to feel the despair from the deaths of my mother, Ema, and Zola that I had been blocking these last five years. It was an emotion I'd never expected, and I don't think I can find the exact way to describe what it was like when this foreign man with a trimmed goatee and sharp cheekbones, wearing a long wool coat, was reciting the poems. Something moved, something shifted, somehow it seemed he understood me. As his voice streamed through the four languages, the words seeped into me like the music I had always heard at home, music Ema listened to, music my mother had hummed, music that relaxed my father as he changed one record after another on our Victrola Sunday afternoons. The melody of these words, the clear way that Anton was annunciating each syllable, felt familiar, grounded, and so strangely personal. Even though I am more visual and not aural, I remember how I was anticipating the coming intonations as if I were creating them myself. Before Anton finished his lecture, I was stirring to get up—to meet him—putting my wet coat over my arm, stuffing my notebook into my bag.

"How old is he?" I wondered, as I waited. Thirty? Thirty-five? And from the Soviet Union, but here for a few months as a guest lecturer, not a Party member. This took place in 1967, when cultural restrictions had eased a bit, and, finally, the Charles University curriculum was allowing short seminars in literature, poetry, art history, and filmmaking.

He, I soon learned, was 29. I'm not sure what Anton thought of me as he watched an eighteen-year-old girl climb onto the stage, approach him while he organized his papers, and ask him if he'd answer questions, and then suggest they could go to the Tokai Café for coffee. He looked down at his feet as if they might tell him how to say no. I had nothing to ask, I'd hardly thought about poetry, but when he looked up a second later I tilted my head in the direction of the café. He buckled his briefcase, slung the strap around his shoulder, and followed. Later, when we talked about our meeting, he admitted he was lonely and was happy to have someone to talk to.

The second time I met up with Anton he suggested we walk along the Vltava. It was a week after the late March snow, the sun was shining, the water glistened. We crossed the Charles Bridge and descended steps into the Kampa Gardens and sat down on a bench. He told me he hoped to see all of Prague during his stay. He wanted to go to concerts, frequent cafés, take the Sunday river cruise, see museums. Our conversation trailed off as we noticed the two people across from us. A large country woman dressed in a maid's gray serge uniform with white apron, and a small, old wisp of a woman dressed in a threadbare but elegant blue suit, with her hair neatly parted, were sitting together. The maid had her arm around the old woman's shoulder, while the old woman's head rested on the maid's chest as she slept with a smile on her face in the afternoon sun. The maid, head bent to her mistress, stroked the old woman's hair. Around them, children running, river ferries, people strolling did not seem to penetrate their cocoon. Anton and I observed them for half an hour or so, and soon, for me anyway, those moments were more intense than anything I'd felt before. I was aware of my breath, and I could hear Anton's breath through his lips, and I wondered, thinking about how I counted Ema's last thousands of breaths—how many more breaths this old woman in her blue suit had, as her head rose and fell with the breath of the maid's large breasts.

We did not make it up to the Strahov Monastery that day. The old woman woke up with a start, the sun had slipped behind a building, so the maid found a shawl in her bag and put it on the old woman's lap. Anton stood up, took my hand to pull me up, and said that he was sorry but he wanted to return now to his lodging. He felt an urge to write a poem.

On Sunday we walked back over the bridge, past houses and apartments, and then veered into the cherry orchard before ending up on the winding wooded path to the monastery. There was a villa in the courtyard that Anton was curious about. One of his colleagues in his boarding house grew up there. We were winded from walking fast, and soon found the gate around the other side of the grounds, and we walked in. Linden trees were beginning to bud, daffodils in a garden by the gate waved in a breeze that cooled us at the top of the hill. To our right, near the entrance, was a red-stucco house, and over the door a plaster molding of a dachshund. "Oh yes," said Anton, "that's what Jan told me, it's called Dachshund House."

Of course I wanted to tell him about Zola, and I did. Zola barking and jumping to greet me when I came home after school. Zola running in circles, into the kitchen, around the table, back out into the living room, around the couch, onto the couch, jumping off, her front legs before her, her back legs following, and then how she landed and came to me and stood on her hind end, her dachshund paws clawing at my legs until I would sit down and allow her onto my lap.

* * *

Once, on a squeaky tram, Anton said, "These rusty rails remind me of Odessa. Of the tramway outside my bedroom. It used to wake me up." Another time as we waited for a tailor to repair the hem of his coat, he told me that the sound coming from the back room was like the tick of his mother's sewing machine when she slaved away late summers making the black smocks for the Odessa symphony orchestra players.

"It seems like you miss home," I said one evening after he told me how he used to help his father with the sound system for the City Opera productions.

"Maybe it's growing up I miss. My cousin and I used to go to the beach evenings in August. We'd swim out as far as we could, and then turn around when the shoreline of Odessa was dark, but the harbor lights, wavering like a mirage, would guide us back."

Anton spoke enough Czech to conduct his classes, but we preferred to speak to each other in German. We'd both grown up knowing that the less said about politics, the less risk there was of arrest. My friends at the university were cautious, wary that their hope for a law degree might be thwarted by a decision made by the Party members. Anton's guest lectureship in Prague happened in the first reprieve from the grip of communism. I never knew what Anton thought about socialism. I didn't want politics to get in the way of my feelings for him. We shared thoughts about books and concerts we attended. He never asked about my family, and I was too shy to tell him about the tragedies. I didn't want to appear sad. I didn't want to lose my relationship with him.

In those months, which were later called the Prague Spring, cafés were full, waitresses carried trays of beer steins to rowdy men, sausage stands popped up in the Old Town square after years of being forbidden, radios in open doorways blared out the Beatles and rock songs from America, students practiced their parts for plays in the commons. I photographed students sitting in groups, students acting in the outdoor theatre, students carrying banners in protest of public posting of test scores, and the early closing of the cafeteria. I developed the film in our basement, but I didn't have the nerve to make prints. I hid the filmstrips in my mother's technical photography books.

*   *   *

Anton and I were on a train heading to Caslav for a long weekend. His friend Jan recommended we start from the center of the village and then walk to a ruin of a castle Anton had heard about, but the train chugged to a stop in a hamlet, and we were told that because of a track situation, it would not go the rest of the way. I suggested we take a train back to Prague but Anton was determined to have this chance to be in the countryside. We gathered our rucksacks, descended the train, and started to walk following signs to Caslav. I couldn't keep up, I had to take long strides. At times I slowed down but then I saw that he was unstoppable; I ran to catch up. He seemed not to want to understand my German as I pleaded with him to wait. He looked back at me, then at the darkening sky, and mumbling in Russian, continued. Just before dusk we found a Gasthaus. All evening I could not shake my mood. It was the first time I felt angry at him. The next day we found the castle closed.

What I didn't understand about him then—we argued

about it on the train back—was Anton's lack of trust for a democratic future. I dreamed of traveling as soon as communism had disappeared—which I hoped would happen soon—and suggested we could travel around Europe and Asia, as I knew Swiss students were doing; some even managed to come to Prague. Anton looked at me. He dropped his eyes. He did not believe in these hopes. He said he counted only on the present, the dawn and dusk and the moments in-between. His sense of the present was the basis of his trust in poetry; he could memorize and make poems privately. Words were what he trusted. He was free to shape them in his mind when and as he liked. He did not rely on vague notions of change but on his creativity.

*   *   *

One day there was a strong knock on our door, followed by pounding. I was alone in the kitchen, trying to fry chicken the way Ema used to do but the chicken was sticking to the pan. The raps were followed by voices saying, "Open the door." I opened it. A man in the Soviet uniform worn by Communist officers handed me a piece of paper. I didn't take it. I knew what it said. Loti's family had received that same order last year. The tall officer pressed it into my hand. "You have a week to move out of the house," he said, as he pushed through the door, followed by the other officer. They walked through the house, their boots clopped through the living room, up the stairs and back down, while the smaller officer checked off on his clipboard what was to stay: beds, tables, couches, armoires, chairs, mirrors, the oil painting above the fireplace, china, glasses, pots, pans, rugs, fireplace tools, linen hand towels. They did not go to the third floor and they did not go into the basement. My father, who dabbled in restoring small paintings since he was no longer at the museum, was spared their interruption.

"Make sure it is presentable," the officer said, as he put the typed command for our relocation on the front-hall table. Above signatures and the Czech Communist Party red-ink stamps, it stated that Johan Karel was to move back to his family cottage in Mimon, and that Maria Karel was to report to the university housing office to register for a room in a boarding house; the room fee would be covered by the State.

I wanted to accept Anton's offer to help, but Papa would not allow it. In spring, when I had mentioned that I had a poet friend from Odessa, he had asked me not to bring him to the house, he could not accept a Russian into our lives. I was numbed by our having to move as thoughts about Anton—our city walks, talks, beers in cafés, reading poems he recommended, dreaming of someday meeting him in Odessa—filled my mind.

Papa, who shortly after the death of Ema had been fired from his thirty-year job as head of restoration at the National

Museum, now seemed distant. He didn't answer me right away, he no longer would eat meat, he didn't want to take walks. After Mama died, he had lost his smile, his warmth. But the deaths of Babicka, Ema, and Zola intensified his depression. I didn't know how to relate to my father about this move, and I had to find the energy to make it happen. I had a vague hope Papa might improve once in the countryside, where he'd at least be away from Prague memories, but I worried that night, as I was trying to fall asleep for one of the last times in our house, that his childhood memories or his sadness for how his mother had struggled at the end of her life, might overwhelm him. He now walked with a cane. He often called me Lydie, confusing me with my mother, and sometimes he sat for hours in his studio staring at the wall. He stirred the food on his plate, paced in his room at night, and went out without a jacket on cool nights and sat on the front steps until I could convince him to come in. I knew I could not impose on him Anton's willingness to help.

The next day I started to pack. I made piles. I tried not to fall as I teetered down the steps with clothes, pillows, quilts. Friends, Helena and Magda, found boxes at the grocery. They stacked the paintings along one wall, carried towels from the linen closet, boxed up the flour and sugar and Ema's spices, and made categories of books for me to choose from. Papa remained in his studio during those five days, unwilling to take part, unwilling to accept that Milan, Helena's boyfriend, and I would load into Mama's Skoda our belongings to take to the cottage on what used to be his small family farm.

Once installed at the cottage, Papa went directly to his old room and climbed into bed. The house was dark, the floors dusty, blue mold lined the sink and the tin shower floor. Everything seemed disgusting. I hated the smells. I had no idea where to start. I didn't want to start. Packing the house had been enough. It rained all week and with windows open to air, water beaded on the sills. I felt apathetic, the task was endless, my emotions on the edge of my eyelids. I forced myself to keep moving. I carried boxes that were now soggy from humidity. One broke apart, and books fell from the bottom; another collapsed, and pans and wooden spoons clattered onto the table; a folder of my mother's negatives fanned out on the floor. I worked for a while, then sat down, then stood up again to bat away at cobwebs. I separated sheets from blankets, placing them over years of dried-up insect and mouse droppings. I took bread and soup up to my father, all the while opening and closing windows according to wind shifts and rainfall.

The second evening, I sat down on Milna's milking stool and brooded. Grass had never grown back over the patch where she used to moo and lie in the afternoon shade. Then a donkey brayed, and another brayed back. I did not belong there. I was a university student, not a hausfrau, not a farm girl. Soon I became aware of someone whistling. The melody filled me with nostalgia until I gathered it was getting closer, until I realized it was Anton, and then there he was, just off the local train, walking up the last stretch of the road.

We talked all evening. He had brought wine and sausages. He slept in the barn. I tiptoed back up to my room at dawn. When morning light beamed onto the grime in the house, Anton made me start over. Everything came off the shelves, chairs were pushed to the side of the living room so floors could be swept with my grandmother's twig broom and mopped with old towels, fireplace ashes were scooped into a bucket. After I scoured the stovetop and stood back to admire my effort, Anton poured soap flakes into the sink water, dipped and wrung out his rag, and scrubbed the burners.

"How do you know how to do this so professionally?" I asked that night as we sat in the overgrown garden watching the sun set. I had pictured him as an aloof family member, reading books, walking the streets with friends, avoiding his parents' apartment by lingering at the university. "My parents," he answered. "And respect for the little we have."

"There's a use to menial chores," Anton announced, when he stacked wood by the fireplace. "I can memorize poetry or think about books when shining my father's shoes or waxing the table."

The next evening while at the kitchen table Anton poked at the dripping wax and said, "Maria. A strong name: Maria Magdalena, Maria Theresa, Marie Antoinette, Marie Curie, Maria Feodorovna. Who is the Maria in you? Who will you become? What will you believe in thirty years from now? How will you spend your life?"

In the morning, we heard the door of Papa's bedroom creak open, heard his feet on the floor above, and watched as he appeared in pajamas with hair wild around his face. Anton rose from the kitchen table bench, bowed his head and extended his hand. Papa stood by the landing for a minute or two, his gaze fixed on the open window, the curtains filling with puffs of air. I had told him the night before that Anton had come, about the work we'd done, but it was clear that my father's feelings formed months ago had not changed. He would not tolerate a Russian in his house, and he would not step forward to shake Anton's hand.

Anton walked to the door, opened it, stepped out as if to get firewood, but instead of pausing at the shed, he strode away from the house and into the darkening night.

"Let him go," my father said. "The decent thing for him to do. A foreign man in the house of a young woman is wrong. A man not invited." My father came into the kitchen, stabilizing his balance by holding onto the back of the chair. I turned and left and ran down the road, calling Anton. I was not wearing shoes, and at first I didn't feel the pebbles on the path, but stones on the dirt road stabbed my arches. Anton was close enough to hear my voice, but he didn't turn around. I was mortified by my father, and could not believe that Anton would just leave without saying something. My left foot hurt from stepping on something like metal or a shard of glass. I had to stop. I had to go back.

*   *   *

When I saw Anton the following week in Prague, I didn't mention what happened with my father. When Anton had to return to Odessa at the end of August to begin his teaching apprenticeship, I didn't yet know I was pregnant. I wrote letters to his post box at the university. I tried to call, but the letters were not answered, and the phone line had been changed. He mentioned he could be transferred to Minsk, and that if that did happen he'd possibly live with his brother, but that idea had seemed unlikely so he didn't give me an address. When I suggested that I'd come visit him, he said not to plan on anything, he was sent where he was sent by an official mandate, and that was that. Seeing me upset, which I was those last few days, made him uncomfortable. He said we were too young to make promises, I was too young to know my emotions. He felt I was not being smart about our diverging destinies. He had a career he needed to be serious about. "Maria," he said, "remember that letters in

Russia are opened and scrutinized. They often don't get to their destination."

*   *   *

It was snowing when I returned for a visit with my father in February. He did not yet know I was pregnant. I was pregnant the last two times I had come, but could not find a way to tell him. I arrived on the night train. There was a charcoal smell in the air. "The barn burned," my father said. He stood at the kitchen window and looked out into the winter. "A storm." He was not sure when it started. The sheep were at the collective, where they spent winters; only a neighbor's old plow horses had been inside. "The wind howled," he said, and then told me that the snow had piled higher and higher under his window, the fireplace flue knocked. During the night, light burned through the storm. It got brighter, like a blurred sunset in a misty painting. Fire flamed on the hill. He said that he got up from bed, pulled on rubber boots and his coat. He stepped into the snow, his boots filled, ice froze around his feet. He took another step and another and fell. The shingle siding of the barn crackled, flames lapped the stone silos. He told me how he had walked up to the barn in the afternoon to give the horses hay, and listened to them moving around in their stalls, and he mentioned to me how clouds of their breath rose in the cold air, their muzzles were covered in hoar frost. He had a sense of something wrong in the barn, so he opened the doors to the corral. He didn't know if they stayed or ran from the flames.

Then he sat down at the table and lamented how peasant life was not as writers and painters and poets depicted. The cold was cruel in winters, with drafts from leaks in windows and floorboards. The summers were cruel with flies buzzing in stale and stagnant air, and then there were the cruel thunderstorms and rains and floods. And now farms were broken and had meager vegetable gardens and small patches of land for crops. And yesterday's dawn especially was cruel. That black and white landscape. The silo alone on the hill.

His voice quavered, the sparkle had gone out of his eyes, had been gone since he was removed from his job. Every day his energy drained, it seemed almost visibly pooling at his feet, making every motion harder, as if he were wading out into the shallows of a brackish lake, not knowing when the muddy bottom might fall away. His eyes traveled across the kitchen, landing on the shelf of chipped pitchers his mother had collected, and then at last he looked at me, into my eyes before he noticed my swollen stomach. He shook his head in what I assumed was disbelief, shock, and shame.

My father found a family cradle in the shed. For days it was perched on the kitchen table on an oilcloth as he cleaned it, sanded it, polished it, sanded it again, and then put on a final coat of varnish. I had come now to stay at the cottage.

We established a routine and he seemed happy I was there, smiling when I came in the door after a walk, making fires to warm me, standing with a towel in his hand when I was washing up after dinner. You were born on a clear spring day in a little clinic outside of Prague. I can't begin to be able to tell you how it was to meet you, you whom I had been carrying inside of me, in spite of the loneliness of losing Anton and not being able to share my innermost feelings with my father, the man closest to me in life. A nurse at the clinic, Emilia, helped me during the last weeks, and she arranged that I stay for a week after the birth. She was there every day, cheery, bringing me bouquets of spring flowers, sugar-braided bread, a hat she had knitted for you. The sun in my room illuminated the white walls, the porcelain sink, the white of the hospital crib. Your cheeks were pink, your eyes would open slowly, and you'd gaze up at me, and I of course could not stop looking at you. Those first days, the following weeks, the next months are memories I've sealed up perfectly like a winter scene in a globe that I need only rotate in my hand and feelings fall like snow.

You filled my longings. Holding you, feeding you, sleeping next to you. My father rocked you when I cooked dinner. It was now the end of May, spring had come to the countryside. In the mornings, my father bundled you in blankets, walked you around the garden to show you the bird feeder, the woodpile, the chopping block. He took your hand in his so he could help you touch the bark of a tree, or feel the feathers of a chicken, or immerse your fingers in the rainwater that had collected in a pail.

* * *

One evening, as I was feeding you in the living room, I heard the wood creak from the upstairs landing and then a crashing sound of something opening. I put you on the rug and walked to the bottom of the stairway. My father had lowered the attic ladder. Dust filtered into the hall as he was rummaging around. Boxes fell, trunks rattled as they were being moved. By the time he came back down, raised the ladder, and disappeared into his room, I was distracted with running your bath. After I tucked you into your cradle, my father appeared in the doorway and said, "I could die anytime. I'm not well. Go to the attic now and bring down the cardboard tubes and boxes. I will sit by the little girl."

I went up the stairs, pulled down the trap door, climbed the ladder, and brought down three tubes and two flat boxes. I dusted them off on the landing and put them onto the kitchen table. When I opened the first box, I saw they were photographs and imagined they were my mother's or were the ones she had collected from her friends, but as I lifted the tissue paper, I recognized immediately that they were by Josef Sudek, who was just becoming famous in Prague.

I turned them over, and there was his signature, the dates, and the name of his first studio. There were twenty still-life photographs in the first box and three of the tree series he took in Moravia in a second box. I could hardly believe that I had been to Sudek's studio, and here were prints from his first edition in my hands. The third box was full of the series "Flowers in Vases" that my mother had photographed before she and my father were married in 1947.

I pulled the contents out of the first tube. There were woodcuts, etchings, and sketches of all sizes carefully wrapped in velum. Some were watercolors. There was a lithograph and a watercolor by Egon Shiele. I flattened them with our iron on one end and a heavy pot on the other, and opened the second tube to find that there were more prints—all of them dating from before the war. My father collected when he was a student and apprentice in Vienna, but I had no idea that he had prints from known artists.

Absorbed in this discovery, I forgot about you and my father. But then you cried, and I ran from the kitchen into your room. You just wanted to be picked up and stopped crying when I held you. My father was asleep in his chair.

Only you made me happy that summer. Papa studied his art books all afternoon and went to bed after dinner. Helena and Milan had promised to visit but then did not find the time. There were no letters from Anton. I wrote a journal about you for him for a few weeks, with the hope he'd walk back up the road and into our lives. You chortled when I tickled you, you ate bananas and cereal, you were comfortable on a blanket under the apple tree, watching clouds float by. I knitted you a hat for winter and made curtains for your room. I cut up a linen sheet I found in a trunk, sewed hems and embroidered your first name and birthday on them, and used them to cover you to keep away the flies. But you kicked them off, your legs peddling the air.

My father and I spent evenings looking at the art. Once the prints were flattened, they were easy to sort through. We put them in the living room, laying them on every surface, creating our own gallery. During some nights, my father got out of bed—he had moved to a little room on the ground floor—opened the door, and tiptoed into the living room. On cool nights he built a fire and brewed tea. I heard the kitchen door closing, or a window being opened, or something being knocked into. The next day the prints had been moved; ones I'd not paid attention to were now in the pile on the table; sometimes he lined up the photographs on the long shelf, mixing Sudek's with my mother's, curating his own series. He put the woodcuts on the mantelpiece—the paper was thicker and remained upright. Sometimes I heard him muttering. One dawn I woke up and heard a wheezing sound. I came downstairs and listened outside the door. He was sobbing the long deep sobs a child makes at the end of a crying spell. "Are you okay?" I whispered. He stopped crying, did not turn to look at me, but in a backhanded motion shooed me away.

In tales that got repeated or mixed up, my father told me about artists, galleries he frequented, how he had saved money, how, after official museum trips, when he returned from Vienna, he had brought the pieces he was able to buy on his own back here to the farm to his mother, to store in the attic. Sometimes on these evenings he found a sketch and placed it on the kitchen table. Or he left one on a little stand by my bed, and then the next morning he took it away. Or for a few days, he stacked the prints in piles on the table and covered them with a cloth. He smiled as he made his arrangements, and the ticking of his head made me think he was reliving the moments when he had been negotiating to buy the pieces, though in reality it was his illness that caused it.

* * *

Papa became insistent that I go to Vienna soon to sell the art. We needed funds now that some of the constraints of communism appeared to have lessened. In spite of whatever illness had set in, he was clear that we needed to start a legal process to reclaim the house in Prague. He wanted me to rent an apartment there in the meantime. "The countryside is no longer a place to raise a child," he said.

I could not take you with me because I couldn't get you a birth certificate. I was still dreaming that Anton would come back and give you his name. The nurse, Emilia, had to go to Brno for the first day of my trip, so she persuaded me to leave you with her cousin. I was not happy about that, as I hadn't met her cousin until that morning. But when I left you with her, you smiled when she held you, and since I was only going to be gone for a few days, just long enough to make a contact to sell the art, and I knew Emilia would be back, I talked myself into the arrangement.

I had the paperwork for the art organized: my passport, proof of purchase for the art, address of a hotel, name of the woman—Frau Müller—who would be my contact. Frau Müller said I should come right away, that the Wiener Künstmesse was going to take place in October. She would need time to sort, photograph, and catalog the pieces appropriate for the fair, but she would be on vacation until August 15. We could meet on the nineteenth. She gave me the name of a small hotel on the Graben near St. Stephan's Dom. "There'll be lots for you to see. I'll leave names of places to visit. You'll get a feeling for Vienna."

In the train, I took out the only photo I had of you and stared at it. When the train neared the border, six Czechoslovak guards stepped from the tarmac onto the train. Guns in their holsters knocked against the corridor. Their fat fingers flipped through the pages of everyone's passports. They searched under seats, patted people's coat pockets, asked the woman across from me to open her purse. One guard took my passport from me, walked down the aisle to talk to another guard, pointed at something in it—my picture maybe—and conferred with yet another guard before coming back, taking the stamp out of his holster, and stamping it. They did not ask about the tubes and boxes I had stored in the overhead rack. Then minutes later, the Austrian guards came through the train. They looked at me, and perhaps saw my fear. One guard said, *"Keine Angst. Hier ist man frei!"*

It was four-thirty in the afternoon on August 19, 1968, when my train pulled into the Hauptbahnhof in Vienna. I settled into the Kaiserin Elisabeth Hotel, walked around the room, ran my fingers over the glistening chestnut dresser, looked at the tiled bathroom and at the claw-foot bathtub. My footprints sank into the carpet. There was a television and a radio on the dresser and a telephone—the most important detail. I placed a call to Czechoslovakia. The hotel operator said she'd ring the room in a few minutes or so. I rested on the feathery bed cover. Outside was the city: bells of tramcars, the six o'clock bells of the St. Stephan's Dom, the clinging bells of bicycles. When the call came through, Emilia, who was back on duty, reported that all was well, you were having your bath, you had loved the afternoon walk in the park.

I walked the length of Kärtner Strasse past stores selling many colors of wool; store windows with mannequins dressed in formal hunting clothes, holding shotguns in one hand and a clutch of pheasant in another; and stores with wedding dresses on thin mannequins. There were cake shops and tearooms. When I went to the Ringstrasse—the wide palace-lined, tree-lined avenue my father had been trying to tell me about—a group of middle-aged people my parents' age, dressed in long gowns and black tie, were coming out of the Sacher Hotel. I followed them down the block until they went up the three short steps to the Opera House.

Frau Müller, wearing a skirt with matching jacket, stockings, high heels, lipstick, and red nail polish, with her hair coiffed in a blond bubble, threw her arms up in the air in greeting, and then pulled out a ring of keys from her purse to unlock the door of the gallery. "You're on time!" she said in a clear German I easily understood, and then she took the tubes and boxes from under my arms. We spread the prints out on long tables. I tried to place them in an order my father would have approved of, while she looked, concentrated, and did not say anything for a long time. She moved the prints around, and left the photographs in the box. She said, "Very good collection. We might sell it as a whole."

"There's a story here," she told me later over coffee. "In fact, there are a few stories. The first, your father, his passion, his collection. The second, prints left in an attic for years. The third, Czechoslovakia, that the borders are open, and many of the etchings and watercolors have come back to the place from which they came.

"Now," she said without giving me any choice, "go along and discover Vienna. Tomorrow I'll pick you up and we'll go to my childhood home. I have to spend the night with my mother so that she can sign a document. It's a beautiful drive. My mother will enjoy having someone young around. We live on a lake in the mountains."

Frau Müller's chalet with green shutters was on a hill with views of the water and mountains. My room was in the eave. I slept under the down duvet without waking once. Her garden was full of roses. We ate breakfast at an iron table set with linen napkins and teacups. A maid brought us boiled eggs and toast. It reminded me of our Prague garden, how we used to have coffee and Kaiserbrot on our terrace, how Ema used to tell me about her childhood. After breakfast, Frau Müller insisted I explore. I took a walk on the path around the lake. A woman was rowing along the shore, her oars dipped and then dripped. Small sailboats tacked back and forth in gusts of wind. The water was blue.

When I returned, Frau Müller was sitting in the study, the radio was on, a frantic voice was making an announcement. Soviet tanks from Poland, Hungary, and the Soviet Union had invaded Prague. Two hundred thousand troops had entered the country during the night. The Soviets had taken over the airport, were shutting down the trains, and were threatening to close the borders the next day. The radio voice said that thousands of people were attempting to flee the country before it was too late. Others had decided not to return. Stores were closing, students were being arrested, proclamations for a return to the Marxist-Leninist rule were being issued. All those who demonstrated anti-Soviet sentiment would be arrested, a period of Marxist-Leninist "normalization" would follow.

I sat down on a chair. Frau Müller looked at me. I saw the concern on her face, the confusion, the anger. I didn't know what to think, did not yet understand the consequences, did not yet feel panic. We listened to the report again and then she said, "Maria, I don't understand. Let me take you back to Vienna where we can see television coverage. They have closed some of the borders. It is not clear what's going on. They're reporting that Czechoslovak citizens will need permits to return. It might be difficult for you to go back." I looked at her with an uncontrollable surge of anger, at this woman telling me I might not be able to go back. I stood, felt faint, sat back down. "I have to go back," I said as the gravity of the voice on the radio sunk in. "I have to go back today."

There was a traffic jam coming into Vienna, another one near the train station. I insisted I leave right away. Frau Müller didn't want to drop me alone while she looked for a place to park; I wept, my head turned, my hands hiding my face. She said I should get in line, she would be there as soon as possible. The lines at the Hauptbahnhof wound around and around the waiting area. People were weeping; others came back from the booth to report that the "visas" were really "permissions," and the trains were running only to the border, and that the borders between Austria and Czechoslovakia were closed because there was going to be a transfer of border guards from the Warsaw Pact coalition that would not be in place for two days. Telephone lines had been cut, radio stations shut down, gas stations were closed.

Frau Müller took me to her apartment, cleared out the books and clothes she stored in her guest room, insisted I drink some soup, and gave me a glass of wine. I told her about you, Zofie. "Maria" she said, "we do not all live perfect lives. I am not married anymore. There was no love. I drifted. My husband left me with nothing. I do not exist anymore for him..."

Two days later I got on a train in Vienna. It stalled for five hours on a siding before nearing the border. At the border there was an announcement that there'd be an overnight delay before the passport control would check passports. At dawn the next morning I was woken up from the uncomfortable sitting position when the door of our compartment was thrust open. The passengers, terrified they'd not be allowed back into Czechoslovakia—there were rumors that anyone with any kind of "record" would be turned away—were eerily quiet all night. A border guard had in his hand a list of the passengers who had boarded in Vienna. He called out the names of those who were to get off and wait in the "station." My name was the fifth called. It was all wrong, I knew. "I am a mother," I pleaded. "I have to be allowed to be with my child." The guard looked at me—a nineteen-year-old girl, a small bag in my hand, hair messy, hastily parted, tears streaming down my face. He read: "Entrance for dissidents who have exhibited anti-Soviet behavior will not be allowed."

I waited in lines, I walked around in Frau Müller's apartment in a fog, I lost my appetite, I shook so hard I could hardly write. Again and again I dialed Emilia's number, but it remained disconnected. I called the clinic; they claimed they were not allowed to give out information about their employees. I called Vaclav, the young man who had come to check up on my father for the days I was to be in Vienna, to get him to go to Emilia's apartment. The first time he went, there was no answer at the door. The second time, he found out that a family had just moved into it; they'd been assigned the apartment when the husband had been relocated to that neighborhood. My knees wobbled. I suffered from vertigo. I spent nights on the floor, crawled into the bathroom, felt sick, crawled back onto the rug. I was entangled in fears that I could not articulate in my mind, fears of a distorted world that was shutting down around me. Every breath, every gesture, every thought stabbed me. Memories scraped, scratched, stung. I was a political refugee, unable to travel out of Austria. I had to report to the Viennese Einwandern Abteilung office once a week, with proof of work and residence.

I moved like a robot and could do only as Frau Müller suggested. She found a small, furnished apartment for me, where I, like the other tenants, could use the garden. She got me a part-time job working at the OstLicht Fotografie Zentrum. She bought me pants, dress shoes, a skirt, and gave me some items she claimed she no longer needed: a purse, two belts, a raincoat, and odds and ends for the apartment. I thought only about you. Smell of your skin, fingernails I trimmed, fluff of hair I brushed. I was afraid of the mirror in my room, so I didn't dare glance at it. The silvery surface was so alive, so much like what I imagined of the Black Sea, Anton's sea of

Odessa, I was afraid he might appear like a mirage and start swimming toward me and then turn around to swim away, as he did on summer evenings of his youth. Even the sound of the clock hurt me, each tick a reminder that the gears were moving and that I might not see him again. Or you. He never knew about you. What are you like? A mixture of us? My reddish hair, his aquiline nose, my freckles, his long fingers, my medium height, our thin limbs, his smile? Or his love of words, my fears, his acceptance of where he came from, my loss of the past?

I felt remorse when I found myself noticing the beauty of the falling of evening light, or sleeping without dreaming about you, or looking forward to the boiled egg I made myself for breakfast. I looked forward to the night, to the dark bedroom. I sat on the edge of my bed, as still as I could be, and concentrated on what I remembered about you. The sounds you made, your smile, your fingers reaching out, wanting to touch something beyond yourself. When I attained that awareness, I was calmer.

Frau Müller asked me to help her photograph a series of prints she was organizing for a show in Berlin, and when she went to Berlin for a long weekend, I worked in her gallery. The Viennese men who came to art shows were dressed in suits; the women wore hats and patterned dresses. The leather of their purses matched their shoes, the silk scarves had designs with race horses and horse bits. They walked in the gallery as if they owned everything, laughed at each other's jokes, commented about the art as if commenting about friends they knew. It was a contrast to my world, now frayed by communism, a window to what my life might have been like had it not been interrupted by Communist ideology. These handsome young men and women shook hands. The men kissed the hands of older women. It would be these people who'd buy my father's collection of prints from Sudek, my mother's mentor, the photographer I had been studying.

The OstLicht Fotographie Zentrum offered a photography class on the weekend. Because I had been given a job not out of merit, but compassion, I made sure I was ready to help. The first months I cleaned the darkroom after the weekend class, and during the week I helped sort and catalog the files of photographs in the archive. It was snowing one morning when I woke up and looked out the window at the heavy branches. I rose out of bed, dressed, ate breakfast. I went outside and walked through the blanketed neighborhood, past statues of Mozart and Beethoven covered with white helmets. I looked at bird tracks, listened to the pine trees creaking. Trams passed, iron wheels squeaked, men shoveled sidewalks. I walked into the side door and stomped my boots. I needed to warm up, to get my hands dry enough to put on the white cotton gloves so I could begin to look through the box of photographers' early photos, to sort them by date and subject matter. The curator of the photography collection, Herr Freilicher, startled me from my concentration and said, "Maria, this weekend there will be a portrait seminar. Would you have the time to model for them? It is only for two hours on Saturday. Wear a black sweater if you have one. The school pays extra for those hours." I had been spending the last five months hoping not to be noticed, and now, with this suggestion, I worried that my shame might be detected. I looked at the prints as he addressed me, but before I could give in to my reticence, I said, "Yes, I have time."

I did not let myself think about the session. The snow continued for the next two days. Life in Vienna slowed down a bit, as it had in Prague, but when it snowed in Czechoslovakia, very few of the old cars ventured out, the streets were often empty. Here, black Mercedes sedans plowed through the foot of snow on back streets that had not yet cleared. By Saturday the snow was packed, the air colder, the sun shining. I walked to the OstLicht as I had done all week, but this time I was more aware of my surroundings and I was beginning to accept that at least being present was normal. As I neared the Zentrum I noticed a man in a blue anorak crossing the street. He was tall, striding along in hiking boots.

Herr Freilicher greeted me. "I'm glad you can be here." Together we moved the wooden platform to the north side of the room. He placed a white shawl and a black one on a table near the chair I was to sit on. He told me that there were only four signed up for the session. The snow had kept people home. Once the session started, I noticed that the photographers were concentrating on the assignment and probably only saw me as a medium to express something about themselves. I felt invisible. They took turns requesting me to look one way, wrap either the white or black shawl around my sweater, turn my upper body. They conferred about color zones, overexposing the film to achieve smooth skin tones. One woman had me look right into her camera and hold back my thick mane of hair. The man in the hiking boots, I learned, was named Edward. He ducked under and then popped out from beneath the black cloth of his large-format camera. After he took photos of a few of the poses he wanted, he came up to me and asked if I needed water or a break.

When the others went to the darkroom to process their negatives, Edward—still wearing his blue anorak—took his camera off the tripod, collapsed the bellows, unscrewed the lens, folded the view cloth, and placed everything into a leather carrying case. "I'm a beginner at this," Edward said. "I've never used such a big camera before, so I'm sorry it took me so long to load the negative carrier." While he spoke, he walked to the window to open the shades. I remember watching his arm as it reached up to pull the cord, and then how the sun through the panes crisscrossed the wooden floors, the chairs, the table along the wall. "How long have you been here? Your German is very good," he asked. When he told me he was Welsh, I had no idea what that meant—and if Welsh meant a country, where exactly that country was.

*   *   *

Spring came. Edward invited me to spend the afternoon with him. One afternoon became another. I could hardly wait to see him, though I felt guilty for feeling a desire to be with him. We took walks in the Vienna Woods or along the Danube. He carried a camera, photographed what he called natural abstractions: water swirling behind the ferry we took across the Danube, twigs on the forest floor, cloud formations, grasses. The OstLicht rented out darkroom space; he came in the evenings on Wednesdays to print. One of those evenings in the dark room, when I was changing the chemicals, he remarked that he was impressed by my knowledge. We were standing side by side. It felt as if I had known him for a long time.

Edward came to the May opening of Frau Müller's gallery. He wore a blue suit, his blond hair was combed back, he winked at me when he came through the door. That day I had received a letter from my father. His handwriting was barely legible. One of the attendants at the retirement home he had been moved into after the Prague invasion had added a sentence at the bottom, saying that my father was not in pain, but that his heart was weak, and he was suffering from memory loss. It was then that I finally accepted that the cottage would soon be gone, folded into a cooperative or turned into a weekend home for an apparatchik. I had asked the retirement home secretary to make further inquiries about what might have happened to you, but he had no news. I was not feeling happy to be out that night.

I introduced Frau Müller to Edward. Her face lit up. She invited us to dinner. We went to a Hungarian restaurant where two men with violins played gypsy music. Frau Müller ordered trappista cheese, goulash, and wine from Tokai. She and Edward talked about people they knew in common at the university. I sat in silence, my heart beating, as I felt myself shrinking while the two of them regaled each other with childhood memories. As much as I felt indebted to Frau Müller, I was also angry. Had she not been so receptive to my journey to sell the art, I'd not have come when I did. On she chatted about three-day nature walks she took with her parents from hut to hut in the Arlberg mountains, and how she, being plump, dragged along, complaining.

Frau Müller looked at me, noticed how quiet I had become, and I guess in an effort to draw me out of my gloom, asked about my summers. I could not answer her. She turned back to Edward and soon they were talking again, he telling her about teaching, his German boarding school, the walks he took in the Harz Mountains, and how he'd always had a passion for trekking in the countryside. He reported that he'd most likely be posted in Vienna for another six months, teaching forestry at the Bodenkultur department of the university. They laughed at things I did not find amusing: a professor of biology who dressed only in white, an art dealer who wore garlic cloves as a necklace, students who expressed interest in silviculture but who were frightened of sounds in the woods. I feared she'd bring up my past. I was sure he'd not want to invite me again on the walks, and just thinking of that, realizing my eagerness for those invitations, made me blush. I did not want to want anything more than being with you, but I woke up now thinking of him.

The next day, Edward called, said he'd be by in an hour, he had some hiking boots he'd bought for me and hoped they'd fit. We walked from the village of Döbling to Weidling and stopped for lunch at a hut that served sausages. Edward asked about Czech photographers, what supplies they could still get with the restrictions, how artists survived censorship. He was curious about my childhood, what it was like in Prague in those days. He wanted to know about my mother and my father, what their hobbies were, how did they adjust to life in a socialist regime. That evening, as we were waiting for a tram to get back to the center of Vienna, he asked me to describe the photographs that my mother had made, the ones I had mentioned I had brought to Vienna in her collection. "Tell me more about the series, the one of flowers, and the other along the river."

* * *

We began to explore the hinterlands. Edward had an old VW. The windows were stuck open, and often he had to jump-start it on a hill to get it going. Yet the battered gray car managed to take us to the monastery in Melk, to the Romanesque churches in hillside villages, to vineyards on slopes flanking the Danube. We stopped on a few of those Sundays for picnics on the rocks by the river, and after lunch we waded through knee-high grasses in the flood plains. It was then that he began to tell me about Wales, the hilly countryside, the woods he played in as a child, why he became a professor of forestry, and how I should come with him one day to see the sea. I thought of Anton's—your father's—sea, the dream I had clung to during my pregnancy and after your birth of you and me living with him in Odessa. But that image, those held-on memories I had of Anton, were dissolving.

Months passed. I spoke with my father. His voice was barely audible. Then one day the retirement home contacted me. My father had died in his sleep. I reeled again from vertigo.

Edward and I were together often. He was respectful of the moments when I sank into a reverie. In the garden, on chilly days, he put his sweater around my shoulders. He read out loud passages of a book he found interesting. We drove out of the city when we had time. One afternoon, we went to the eastern Austrian farm country. He stopped to consult his map, to look for the ruin of a Baroque chapel he'd been to last year. He wanted to make photographs of the interior arches; the photographs he took before were dark, and lacked definition. He had borrowed a floodlight from the OstLicht. I was to hold the light, as I used to do for my mother. We ended up taking a route Edward had never been on. When we arrived at a fork in the road, and there was a sign that he thought he recognized, he suggested we go on foot the rest of the way. He parked the car, folded the map into his pocket, got out his backpack, stuffed what looked like a large flashlight into it, and handed me my jacket.

The land unfolded, rising and descending through rows of corn and fields of sugar beets. We walked and walked, but the horizon, the crest of the hill where the chapel should have been, appeared out of reach. The road was endless in the afternoon glare. I was tired. Edward decided on a short cut on a tractor path that was rutted from rain and slippery in places. At last we neared where the path must have come to an end. I was catching up when Edward stopped abruptly, as if he realized he had lost the way, as if he had run into a barrier. I walked the last few steps and saw what gave him pause. There, below us, was the mined trench, the wavering grass swath that cradled the ten-foot rolls of concertina wire that stretched along the border from Hungary to Austria to Czechoslovakia to Eastern Germany. I shut my eyes, felt dizzy, and turned to walk off. Edward caught my wrist and held it as we retreated, retracing our steps, walking fast down the path.

*   *   *

The impenetrable border outside of Vienna came between what I had always known and the unknown. It was not until years later in Wales with the birth of Teddy that I started settling down. His birth was not an easy birth. I'd been fearful that I'd never get pregnant again and it took time. I was afraid of miscarrying, of stillbirth, of kidnapping, of something happening those first months. The labor was long and Teddy was jaundiced, and he had to stay in the nursery for days, baking under special lights. I've never felt that my English is easily understandable. At first I was so shy and dependent on Edward and his younger sisters that I didn't make friends, wouldn't allow myself to feel at home, especially those first years when we lived in an apartment above his grandfather's garage. I was displaced. I had Edward, but I was a stranger in this new foggy country. I practiced

English with Mary. I learned about gardening from Julia. I read Julia's books about young English women—women who grew up on estates, women who worked in grand houses as tutors, women who were banished for having affairs—and who they might marry. I had been living with the shame that I was a refugee, a political dissident, whose crime had been photographing the Charles University student sit-ins and marches in 1966, in 1967, and in the spring of 1968. There was nothing I could change about the Communist apparatchiks who found my photographs in the same dark room where my mother had hidden negatives she took of the neighborhood Jews being rounded up in 1942.

In my early days in Wales I took walks in the hills with Edward's father's setters. Edward and I drove to the sea on Sundays for picnics. Edward traveled to Austria, to Germany, and to London to give lectures. He made side trips to Prague. There he walked the streets, knocked on doors, asked my old friends if they had any ideas of how we could find you. He visited hospitals, scoured lists of misplaced people, of people who fled, of people who'd been allowed to return, in hopes that he'd find Emilia or her cousin. Now it has been years since Julia and Mary and Edward and I have been searching for you, sending what seems like useless inquiries to government ministries, letters to orphanages, to schools, to the Czechoslovak census bureau, the adoption bureau, the deportation bureau, the bureau of vital statistics, the bureau of lost family members. Mary, who devoted the most time to doing research, and who'd read about the border closings that came about after the Warsaw Pact invasion, offered that perhaps because the night of August 21 was so terrifying, the woman who had been taking care of you had to go into hiding and possibly left you with a relative, and, now, that is all we can surmise. I lie in bed at night facing the window that opens westward, away from the direction of the miles and miles of barbed wire of the Iron Curtain. Waves crash on the rocks, water spills, there is a moment of stillness I listen for before the current washes the water back out to sea.

ZOFIE
Vacek House
Bohemia

We could hardly speak that first night at the supper table in Brno. The children fell asleep after wandering around the small apartment looking for their parents. Lukas peered under the bed, in the closet, behind the curtains. Nataša sat most of the day on the floor by the dollhouse Georg made for her, sucking her thumb, hugging her mother's pillow, smelling perhaps a last trace of her parents.

We avoided looking at each other, afraid of our emotions and the confusion—or at least that is how I felt, but finally I said what was on my mind.

"What can be done? What about the children?"

Tomas shook his head and shrugged as if he didn't know what to think.

The clock outside struck eleven. After saying goodnight, Tomas slipped through the hall door to the children's room. I heard Lukas's bed creak as Tomas climbed in next to him. I put bedding and some blankets on the floor under the window in the living room, but then, worried about Nataša waking up in the night, I changed my mind and went into the children's room to find Nataša curled in a ball, her body wrapped around the pillow. Without taking off my slacks and shirt, I lifted the covers and lay down next to her.

I am not sure I slept much. I had been afraid to stir Nataša's sleep so I didn't dare turn over. I was aware of Tomas being so close, but oddly, it seemed appropriate that we both comfort the children. During the night Nataša whimpered now and again. I patted her shoulder and told her the first lie I was conscious of saying: "It's okay, everything will be all right."

A knocking on the front door startled me. Tomas, already awake and out of the room, opened it to a middle-aged woman and man pushing—as he later told me—to get in.

"We've come for our grandchildren," I heard the man say. "We were on the train all yesterday. I'm Milos, my wife is Otilie," he said, putting down the bag. "Where are they? It's been almost two years since we've seen them. Katarina invited us, but Georg always said no, that he would bring them to see us."

Tomas led them into the living room, where they collapsed onto the two chairs. I got out of bed, careful not to wake Nataša, and tiptoed to the bathroom to brush my hair.

"They're still sleeping," I said when I introduced myself a few minutes later. Otilie stood up, thrust out her hand to shake mine. She came up to my shoulders, her hair was braided and coiled at the back of her head, her hand was cold, her grip was weak and felt like holding sparrow bones.

"We are simple people, clerks in case you are wondering," she said, as if to apologize for their wrinkled complexions and their attempts to dress for a city: he in pants with suspenders and an unironed shirt with the top button fastened; she in a baggy housedress fastened at the waist with a green ribbon. "Milos has a condition. We have to think of our future before we make rash decisions."

"We are going to take the children," Milos said to her in an annoyed voice. As he spoke, I saw Georg in his facial expressions. He was handsome as was his son. His blue eyes, like Georg's, were beautiful, but he, also like his son, looked at the ground as he spoke. "They have only us. We'll repaint Georg's old room." He looked up and said, "We live in a village. They can walk to school. They are other young children nearby. The country will do them good. We will never doubt what we must do."

"The clinic told Milos he has to retire from the post office, to rest, to live a quiet life. So I will work in the registrar's office again," Otilie said, rubbing her hands, looking first at Tomas and then at me. "Milos is not to pick up heavy things. His back is broken anyway from the detention camp."

"Forget the camp, don't bring it up, Otilie."

"I'll make some coffee," I said. "I'll wake the children while it brews."

But Lukas was already up, hiding in the hall. He ran to Tomas, clung to his leg. Tomas picked him up and walked to Otilie and Milos.

"Say good morning to your grandparents." Lukas hid his face in Tomas's shoulder.

"I want Ma. I want Pa," he said and then he began to cry, which made Otilie cry. Tears streamed down her cheeks and dropped onto her collar. She stood up and walked over to me.

"I will help in the kitchen," she said sniffling. "We do not like coffee. Milos drinks warm milk."

A secretary from Social Services for the Welfare of Children called at ten and said that two officers would be by in the afternoon. When the doorbell rang, Nataša was settled in front of her dollhouse, four of her dolls were sitting around the little table. Milos was asleep in a chair; the sound of his snoring rose and fell and was audible throughout the apartment. Otilie knitted.

"Socks," she said when she noticed me eying her machine-like finger movements wrapping gray wool around a needle. My head hurt. I was exhausted. I didn't care what Otilie was making. I had not yet had a chance to think about anything as Otilie and Milos had taken all of the air out of the atmosphere.

Otilie fretted when she made Milos's milk too hot. They argued about Georg's clothes; would they sort his things this afternoon, shouldn't they give them to the church. Milos discussed packing the children's things, while Otilie shook her head and knitted more ardently. Unabashedly, she broke out crying again. She didn't wipe her face. Lukas wanted only to be held by Tomas. Now and again Otilie tried to engage him with a wave or a smile, which made him cry out, "I want Ma. I want Pa."

When I opened the door to the people from Social Services, there was a pretty, young woman and an older man. They looked around quickly, discreetly, greeted Milos and Otilie, before the woman sat on the floor next to Nataša. The man reviewed the case: cause of deaths, location of the accident, time, and circumstance. He asked questions about our relationship to the children and to the parents. Milos informed him of his intention to take the children. Otilie repeated her thoughts. The man held up his hand, and said, "First things first."

As we sat in the afternoon light while conversing with them, I felt dizzy again. My head and my heart were pounding. The future was being planned. What would happen to the children? I was Nataša's godmother, a role I was not attached to or even understood—not being religious or having had godparents. No will had been left. I assumed grandparents had the right to their grandchildren. Where were Tomas's parents? Too distanced in their own marriage to offer a united front? I noticed how the young woman had begun to play with Nataša. The dolls, two of them in Nataša's hands, two in the hands of the social worker, were in the dollhouse, then outside, then going to bed, then being seated in chairs around a table—living it seemed from one scene that led to the next. Nataša moved hers with a jerking motion, while the young woman's jumped from the bottom floor of the house to the upstairs.

I stood up and said I needed fresh air and announced that I'd go to the market while it was still open. Nataša looked behind her and said, "Can I come too?"

Rather than turning left to go to the stores, Nataša steered me toward the park, but once we got there she didn't want to play with the children. We stood and watched. I did not encourage her. She held my hand, as she has done now and again since she was two.

"Let's sit under that tree for a while."

Nataša climbed onto my lap, put her head against my chest, took a few deep breaths, and began to cry. When I hugged her closer, I found I could not contain my sadness either. She clung to my arm. Our bodies sighed in unison, questioning, in our sobs I suppose, and in some kind of inarticulate way, how two days ago the woman we both loved and both depended on had been alive, and now, where had she gone? How does death take someone away without the slightest warning? Even in the most exhausting or hardest of times there had been color in Katarina's cheeks. In death, her face, and Georg's, I knew, were drained of life. Now they were on planks in a morgue not far from where we were huddled. For a while, I was only aware of our anguish.

Nataša's matted hair, sweaty from crying, was moist against my blouse. I realized in spite of the admiration and affection and envy I had always felt toward Katarina and Tomas, that I had never been in a vulnerable enough place to feel pure sensations as I was experiencing now. For a moment there was a clarity I can't describe, maybe because in a way I felt Nataša and I were sharing the lowest moment one can have in life, while at the same time we had each other. I had used the word love in my mind to describe my feelings about Tomas and absolute devotion to Katarina, but I had never really belonged to either of them. I was the outsider; there were boundaries. Now, the boundaries had shifted.

Sitting as we were in warm heat of the late afternoon, with sounds of children playing, a child on a swing being carried from the shade into the sun, from sun into the shade, the hum of traffic, and frolicking dogs, I thought about how I had always placed Katarina on a pedestal. She was the person I wished I could have been. She was beautiful and a warm friend and a devoted mother. Now that pedestal had toppled, and for the first time, rather than missing her as I had been a few moments earlier, I flushed with an anger that must have been churning in the back of my mind. The crash was an accident, caused probably because Georg had had too much to drink. Or it was caused due to a private argument they could not let go of in spite of their love of the children. In a way, it suddenly occurred to me, their arguments defined them and heightened their individuality within their marriage. Complaints, threats, pleas burst out of them, tore into each other, broke apart their silence that they'd been enduring since the last fight. Katarina stamped her foot, Georg crashed his fist into the wall, or they slammed doors as their anger inflamed, then burned around them, until the burning hurt so much that they lost their grip on what was driving it all, and soon, surprisingly, poignantly, they felt affection for each other again. I remember being aware on a few of those nights of that strange quiet after those arguments when they repented, making love perhaps, swearing to never let it happen again. The next morning I'd notice Georg coming up behind Katarina and putting his arms around her waist as she was washing dishes, or Katarina would make a joke all the while looking at Georg, waiting until he laughed, which he usually did.

A snarling sound made me look up. The playground,

which had been a blur, suddenly came into focus. A terrier had in its mouth a blue-and-red plastic ball. I had been vaguely aware of a tossing game between two children but now could see that one bad throw had sent the ball right into the mouth of the dog. The dog hurled his head back and forth, strengthening its grip on the ball, growling, as saliva flew from his mouth. When an older woman—his owner—tried to get hold of the ball, the dog dodged her as if in a game they'd played since he'd been a puppy. But at that moment there was a screech of the tram as it rounded a bend on the tracks, a sound so piercing that it distracted the dog, and he paused from his attack mode. His owner grabbed the ball and held it above her head. It surprised me that the dog's grip on the ball had been so deadly, as if he had been trying to kill a chicken.

Nataša, perhaps hearing something threatening in the dog's snarls, shuddered between sobs. My thoughts slipped back to the time I was coming home from school one afternoon with one of my headaches when I heard Uršula yelling at Jakub, and how my needs became diminished by her fear that Jakub was demanding something from her that she could not understand or did not know how to give. I thought of the little bedroom I spent my childhood in, the hidden TV guide cutout pictures of women who might have looked like my mother. My thoughts skipped to how I was here in Brno, in a park with my best friend's child in my arms. Part of me hated the dog at that moment. The dog, no doubt loved by its owner: his owner who played cat-and-mouse games with him, offering him something like a rag or a toy to toss around, allowing him his own hunter instincts. I guess I felt a certain responsibility, or lack of it because I could not react, did not rise up to help save the ball from its probable deflation as I normally would have done. I was engulfed in something more devastating. But the interruption upset me. I identified with the ball, and the child who was watching his ball being mauled. But also, I understood the dog was seizing an opportunity, playing with a toy that fell into his realm. I did not feel capable of separating one emotion from the last. I berated myself for thinking like this, for allowing these extraneous thoughts. I guess my own loss had flared into lifelong sorrow; a sorrow I had tried to suffocate, one I never came to understand, but now was feeling while holding this child in my arms. A child who would suffer from her own lifelong sadness.

Later, lying on the floor in the living room under the quilt, the one that I had always used when I had come to visit, I watched the car lights from the street flicker across the walls. Nataša had fallen asleep early. I sensed she would not wake during the night. After dinner, Tomas and I organized the food in the kitchen cabinets, and then I gathered up the nerve to open Katarina's closet, expecting to have her clothes tumble onto me in their normal disarray, but I was wrong. Shirts and pants were neatly stacked and the sweaters were folded. Something had shifted in her recently, I sensed. Whenever I came to visit her, I had to remember that needs of children came before household chores, and the apartment, though hardly livable for me, with chairs tilted into forts, beds unmade, bathtub grimy, was how Katarina kept it. Other than the little that Tomas and I rearranged in the kitchen, I was realizing that Katarina had begun to feel pride in her domestic realm.

I drifted to sleep, wondering what the meeting with Social Services and Georg's parents would be like tomorrow. The social workers had left by the time Nataša and I came back from the park, as had Otilie and Milos. I fell into a dream right away it seemed, but the dream was hard to remember. I drifted in and out and then woke up. In the fleeting images, I had been aware that the dream was taking place in a park with trees and a pond, and there was a dog running toward me, a bigger dog than the terrier, a dog with beautiful glassy eyes; eyes dogs have that make their owners believe in their dog's kindness and loyalty. Presently, I became aware of someone next to me, behind me actually, as I was lying on my side, and as I thought to turn, thinking I was still in a dream or that Nataša had come looking for me,

Tomas said, "It's me. I needed to be next to you. You were sleeping. I didn't want to bother you, but now you're awake. Do you mind?" When I said of course not, Tomas moved closer and put his arm around my waist. We remained silent, afraid perhaps to know what the next moment might offer. I put my hand over his.

"I told the Social Services that you and I could adopt the children. I've been a coward about getting involved. I just couldn't take the step after watching my parents."

I turned toward him, and for the second time that day, I could not control my emotions. As Nataša's tears had unleashed mine, mine did the same for Tomas's. Earlier, while spreading out the quilt to make my bed on the floor, I could not imagine how any of us would be able to face another day with the gloom that Katarina's and Georg's deaths had spread over everything.

When the blue light of dawn crept across the room, I sat up, pulled my blanket around my shoulder, and, noticing that Tomas was awake, said, "I have a job, a contract with the Ministerstvo. You've questioned being involved. Were you serious last night? It wouldn't be fair for the children if you don't love me. If we could adopt them how would I know how to be a mother?"

Tomas sat up, scooted in front of me, looked me in the eye, and said, "I do love you. I always have, I think, but I knew for sure that time you came on your own to the lake and we went out on the boat. You had stopped rowing. We were drifting, watching the ducks. We didn't talk for a long time, and in that silence, something happened, something welled up inside of me. As that peacefulness enveloped us, I recognized how strong you are. Few people feel comfortable sharing moments like that. It took guts for you to come to the lake at all. The emotion was so strong it embarrassed me, so I decided to swim back to the dock. Underwater I knew I wanted to be with you, Zofie."

Since our marriage was in some ways encouraged by fate, we made a point of practicing being present for each other. Tomas was conscientious that we not allow ourselves the alienation that his parents had succumbed to.

"Not now, of course," he said one night after dinner when Nataša and Lukas were settled in their rooms in the Vacek house, "but later when we're tired of what's new about being with each other."

After we had moved to the manor house once the adoption paperwork had been completed, I began to see the challenge not only with how we would be all we could be for the children but also with the upkeep of the house. There were leaks, buckled walls, flues that didn't draw, cracked windows, faded upholstery, broken shutters, and mold. As a way to deal with the steps to repair the house and talk about Nataša and Lukas, it became a habit once the children were settled to return to the kitchen and make plans. After the first few months, and perhaps feeling driven by the needs of the children, which seemed endless and exhausting for me and for Tomas too since we'd both led solitary lives until now, we relied on the relaxing time when we began discussing how to keep the idea of their parents alive in their minds. It was easier to discuss the house renovation: how much money could be afforded for new doors or an oven repair or box springs. The reality was that there was no extra money. Tomas's position at the Plzen Publishing House did not pay well, and I had only just begun to think about how to find freelance work.

On weekends, I could look out a window and see the rake reaching out to the pile of terrace pebbles, then clawing its way toward Tomas as the pebbles burst around the prongs and fanned into place. I'd hear the thud of shovelful after shovelful of dirt filling the wheelbarrow as Tomas dug down into the septic tank to repair a pipe. I'd see Lukas, now three years old, following his uncle, pushing a plastic toy lawnmower as Tomas cut the grass with the sputtering old push mower. Tomas could find me in the old school room—which we'd set up as a shop—sanding a small table, trying to reframe an old mirror, rewiring a lamp. I made an art table out of an old door for Nataša. Using crayons and colored pencils, Nataša filled pages and pages of paper with circles and suns and stick figures. I bought watercolors for her and soon Nataša's paintings became abstract. The colors were beautifully thought out for her young age. She fell into a trance when she painted. "What is this about," I asked when she used soft blues and violets of the watercolors. "A woman," she said, "in a velvet dress."

One afternoon, Tomas came in from his latest project, took the hammer out of my hand, and announced that his father—who lived in the apartment adjoining the house—was going to take care of the children for a few hours.

"It is this I mean," he said as I followed his orders. "We need to do things for ourselves, by ourselves. Let's go." Tomas drove out into the country in a direction I'd not been. We drove past fields, up hills, down swales. Soon we were in the middle of a forest. "It's been years since I was here," he reflected. "I think I dreamt about it last night. There should be a trail that leads to the ruins of a village."

This was the beginning of what he called "moments." At his insistence we planned one or two a week. "They need not be elaborate or take long or even be excursions," he advised. It took me a while to begin to think of things where we could share some time.

"Your turn," he'd announce.

One summer evening, well after dinner, I told him that

he and I were going to have some drinks and a surprise in the garden. I was six months pregnant and happy to have a reason to relax. I was not used to these gestures of taking breaks; the effort seemed amusing, as if we were meant to be acting out scenes in a play where we had not learned the lines. That night I put a tablecloth on the iron table on the terrace. We had stubs of candles. By the time we both had time to sit down it was dark, and there was only ambient light from the lantern by the door and the flicker of the candles. I had poured a glass of beer for Tomas and cider for me.

"This is pleasant," he said. "It's nice to sit here and listen to the sounds."

I imagined the garden lit up with a string of lights, I'd invite friends for dinner, Tomas would grill sausages. But we didn't have friends yet. Tomas's and my school friends lived in Prague. The house was big and needed life, more children and guests who'd come and stay. Nataša and Lukas, at my prompting—she six, he four—tottered down the steps, each with a plate of cookies. Their profiles glowed in the soft light: Nataša with braids down her back, apron strings trailing, Lukas's cheeks red, as they presented us the cookies, smiling. Tomas took a bite. "Umm. Did you make these?"

NATAŠA
Vacek House
Bohemia

Dear Ma, I can't accept that you are just bones in a box under a stone in the graveyard in a clearing in our woods. Every August 10th, rain or shine, I used to dress in a skirt and an ironed blouse, Lukas put on his jacket and best pants, and we'd all go to your graveside to recite poems or read thoughts to you and Pa. It's too sad to go there alone, even though it's at the end of the garden. Last time I refused to go with the others. It seemed childish for someone who was fifteen, so instead I'm writing this letter to you.

Two weeks ago, when I fell from my horse, I thought I had died, too, because you were there—alive as can be, kneeling beside me. In seconds I realized it was only in my mind. I can't get over how I have been a child without real parents, even with all Zofie and Uncle Tomas offer. Even from that first morning when Zofie arrived to stay after you and Pa died, when she held out her arms, patted her lap, and invited me to lean against her while she read storybook after storybook.

I used to have nightmares. Scenes flared around the edges, like burning paper. I tossed, turned, would sit up, lie back down. I kicked the covers off. When I was younger, Zofie came. "Nata (she calls me Nata rather than Nataša), it's all right, it's only a dream. Open your eyes." And after I'd wake up she'd say something like, "Look out the window. Is the moon up? Let's see how many stars we can count." She'd sit on the side of the bed, hold my hand, and talk about her times growing up with you. She'd tell me about her childhood, how lonely she had been, how she wished she could at least picture her mother. One night she said, "We have the right to be sad sometimes. There are so many questions we'll never be able to answer." She smelled like cold cream on those evenings, her loose hair fell over the heart patterns of her flannel nightgown.

I wonder how you'd feel if you could see us—this cobbled family that Zofie and Uncle Tomas created with Lukas and me after you and Pa died—living in your old ancestral house. How hard Zofie works to bring this place back to life. She organizes and reorganizes the bookshelves. She refinishes and repaints furniture—side tables, dressers, chairs—from the attic. She polishes silver tureens and glass collections. She hired retired Vacek Glass Works employees to powerwash the façade and two Roma sisters in matching red skirts to re-cover chairs and sofas and to hem the curtains. She organizes all of this in the morning before we are up, before a day burrowed in her office where she translates literary articles and German novels into Czech.

After dinner, when Lukas and I have gone off to do our homework and Grandpa Otto has gone to his rooms and Zofie has said goodnight to Kata, Uncle Tomas and Zofie often return to the table to talk. One night last week I stayed up and was making a sketch of the dogs while listening to their conversation as they talked about what needed attention. Zofie sighed and stated that if they fixed up the upstairs maybe Uncle Tomas's brothers and families would visit more often. She was always commenting how fun it would be to have the house full, and she mentioned that the tourist bureau in Plzen called about the possibility that they'd offer rooms a few weekends later this spring and in early summer for hikers or people driving though Bohemia.

I go to the same school you went to, as does Kata. Kata, my nine-year-old sister—or is she my cousin since she is really Uncle Tomas's and Zofie's child? I will never forget the birth and the sudden death of their first daughter. It was a few years after they got married and we had come here. I can still picture them holding Vera, or rather how Uncle Tomas, at that horrible moment when it was clear that the baby was dead, held

Zofie as she clasped Vera to her chest, and how finally Uncle Tomas had to take the stiff baby from Zofie's arms. Zofie fell forward in her chair and cried. I thought she had been stabbed, the way she curled around what was no longer there. I sensed the bottom of her sadness. Her tears scared me. Zofie has ways for making any bad time better. When Lukas and I used to argue, Zofie would clap her hands together and suggest a game. When we were younger it was hide and seek, now it's card games she learned from your grandmother, Maticka, when she went with you to the lake house. When I saw her cry for Vera, I realized that she might not ever be able to get over the pain of her two-month-old baby dying—for no apparent reason—in her crib. I understood that she might not cry for me in that same way. Her daughters are, or Vera was, and now Kata is, her *own*. I have no *own* other than Lukas.

I watched Zofie's face become serene when she used to rock Kata to sleep. Kata and Zofie hold hands when they walk up the path to school. Zofie smiles and tilts her head as Kata tells Zofie one of her endless made-up stories. I notice every time Zofie buys Kata things: dresses, shoes, bows for Kata's hair. Even though I often think about how Zofie, too, did not know her mother, I can't know what that was like for her. I am not sure she was affected that much because she is happy most of the time. I know all she wants is for me to be normal, but I am becoming different. Something inside of me is pulling me down. It's a voice that says no. Before, I could smile even when I didn't want to, now I can't. I used to go along with any plan. Now it's hard to talk about bad dreams or bad feelings. I'm not in the mood to help around the house. I just want to be in my room and have the time to paint or draw. I should express how grateful I am that we have horses, but I think horses were her dream.

Two years ago Zofie invited Uršula here for the weekend. I wonder if you had met Uršula. She was the woman who raised Zofie in a boarding house about an hour from here. She took me there last when I was ten. I remember the small, plain stucco house that sits alongside a plum orchard. I remember the kitchen table, the little fireplace, the twig-looking chairs in a little room next to the kitchen. The beds were hard in the room Zofie and I slept in. I overheard Uršula whisper into Zofie's ear something about how it was not polite for me to speak up at certain times. I had asked her why she had a stone sink, why there was not a sofa in her sitting room, why she had an ironing board set up in the kitchen, why her cook stove worked only with wood.

When Uršula arrived at our house that weekend, she looked as if she'd put on her Sunday clothes, but her stockings had a run, and her linen blouse was yellowed. Her shoes, though shined, were old, and the heels were so worn that she appeared to rock on them with each step. I could not understand how Zofie, who is slim, has the most beautiful profile, freckles that make her face glow, a lovely smile, looks great wearing matching slacks and sweaters she buys on sale, and can speak four languages and talk with Uncle Tomas about ideas in books—how she could have come from Uršula's simple house. How was she raised by a woman who seems old, and who looks unhappy? Zofie asked Uršula if she might want to live with us. Supposedly she was a good cook—made her own farmers cheese and yogurt and things like that. But she decided to stay in her own house. It was hard to sit next to her at dinner and find something to talk about. She smelled like dried mushrooms. She made lip noises when she sipped her soup. She pulled a handkerchief out of the sleeve of her sweater, blew her nose, and then put it back. I could not think of anything to ask her. And she didn't ask me anything.

Zofie and Uršula cooked. Jelly jars clacked in the pan on the stove. Bread dough swelled under a damp cloth. Dumplings, filled with prune jam, bobbed to the surface of boiling water. They were serious, not laughing and chatting the way Zofie does with us. When it was time for Uršula to go back to her village on Sunday afternoon, she stood on the front steps with her bag packed, scarf tied under her chin, arms around her purse, waiting for Zofie to drive her, without saying anything to me, not even goodbye. I said goodbye but she didn't seem to hear.

Since the full use of the farm has been given back to the Vaceks, Grandpa Otto and Uncle Tomas and Lukas have been working on restoring the gardens and fields. Now linden trees growing in the alley are tall, stumps of statues have been removed, the orchard is producing cherries and plums, the fountain works, and the lawns are irrigated with a flood system from the stream, devised by Uncle Tomas. There are chickens in the coop and pigs in the shed, and my horse, Pavo, and Kata's bay pony, Nico, are in the stable. Lukas adores Uncle Tomas. They've been fixing things afternoons whenever the weather is nice. Grandpa Otto spends time on his tractor scraping smooth ruts in the alley. Uncle Tomas loves chain-sawing dead trees or firewood, or rebuilding a shed. Lukas stacks kindling under a tin roof. Grandpa Otto strolls by to check out the interesting patterns Lukas makes as he stacks the wood, and claims that Lukas, when he grows up, will be an architect.

"Okay," Uncle Tomas said one night when Zofie brought up the idea of making extra funds by accepting occasional paying guests. "It's not like we'll make much from it." I didn't like the idea. It would be extra work. We'd have to be presentable, have our rooms tidy. Zofie claims she'll give them breakfast. She is now correcting me if I don't serve plates on the left side and clear from the right.

"It will be interesting to hear their stories. It could bring something of the world into our lives," Zofie said a few days later. "And Nata, why don't you have some friends for a weekend?" I think she has forgotten about the last time I had Leni and Mina to stay. We were starved at midnight, so we decided to make toast, but then sparks began to fly and the toast caught on fire so I pushed the toaster into the sink and doused it with water. During supper that night, which we ate with everyone in the glassed-in porch, Zofie asked them questions: where did they spend summers, what subjects did they find hard, what were they reading. And Uncle Tomas did too, while urging them to have seconds, and cutting more bread. Had they been to the seaside, did they read the newspaper. Of course they answered, and even seemed to like the questions, when all the while we could have been watching television.

The portrait of your grandmother in the living room is of a girl in a black riding coat. She has blond hair, pink cheeks, and blue eyes. I've tried to copy it because the colors are clear, but people are hard to paint, they don't end up looking like what I intend. But even though their necks are too long, their shoulders sloped, and their eyes too far apart, I think I am getting better at making them look realistic. When I asked Grandpa Otto why there were no portraits of you, he shook his head the way he always shakes his head if the subject of communism comes up or when I want to find out more about you. He explained to me that money from the bank in Vienna had been frozen and that luxury of any kind was forbidden. He told me that he, unlike German neighbors who were forced to leave after the war, stayed on the family farm to try to keep the property intact. The portrait of his mother had been hidden since the beginning of the war when the Nazis marched into Bohemia. A few years ago Zofie found it in the storage shed and asked me to clean it up as best I could. She hung it where for decades there'd been a gray outline on the coral-colored papered wall.

Zofie gave me a book about horses for my birthday. She seemed excited that I would love horses, and, as she handed me the book, she said, "Maybe one day you'll learn how to ride." I thought that riding would seem like a more normal hobby than the watercolor paintings I've been making since I was young. Even though everyone compliments my paintings, and they've been in an exhibit in a gallery, people ask what the paintings are about, and seem confused because the greens and blues and purples of trees or rivers or hills do not look like a copse of trees, flowing water, or swales. I can't explain that I am looking for you in those paintings, and sometimes even begin to imagine you coming out of the woods, or walking through fields, or sitting by the river.

I read in the horse book about draft horses, horses that lived in the marshes in France, Arabian horses, and Lipizzaners. The next morning I walked down to our stables and looked at how the stalls—now full of lumber from fallen build-ings—were arranged with stone water troughs and corner bins for oats. I found Grandpa Otto on his tractor, clearing brush near the woods, and jumped on the sideboard. I asked about the stalls, and who in his past had had horses. He told me it was his mother. In those days there was a groom who slept in the room above the barn. When the war began, my grandmother's horses were taken by the Germans and the groom was sent to the army. Since then, stray cats have had litters of kittens in the stalls. "I'd like to learn to ride," I announced. Grandpa Otto took the pipe from his mouth and laughed. "A good dream," he said.

I overheard Zofie discussing her interest in having horses with Uncle Tomas. "We have the space, and it's good for children to care for animals." One morning I looked out of my window and saw a pony and a gray grazing in the pasture. They were a gift from a neighbor who claimed his wife and daughter had lost interest. An Austrian riding instructor was hired to come once a week to give Kata and me lessons. Kata was a born rider. The very first day, she climbed on, picked up the reins and urged Nico into a brisk walk. The first time I got on, I clutched the saddle horn. In time I became comfortable saddling up and riding at a walk and trot with Kata in the woods. A few weeks ago I was riding alone in the field when I fell off Pavo. I'd been trying to practice smooth cantering transitions but it was hard to make Pavo canter. I kicked him and tapped him with the crop. I nudged my heels again into Pavo's ribs to make him change. Around we went, Pavo trotting faster as I posted up and down, losing the rhythm at times. Then he stumbled and I was thrown onto the shorn corn stalks. I could not at first even breathe. I felt the hard ground and then the sharp stubble. The trees in the nearby woods, the clouds— everything was spinning. But there you were and then you were gone. The break in my leg began to stab. I leaned up on my elbow and saw Pavo heading to the barn, the stirrups bouncing against the saddle, scaring him into a canter.

I had a hard time that night falling to sleep. The next morning the crutches I'd been given after the cast was plastered over my leg were leaning on the bed. On the side table there was breakfast and a vase of daffodils picked by Zofie. The sunlight poured through the petals. The room was bright and warm. Zofie had been with me off and on all night, propping pillows under my leg, bringing me water, cracking the window for air. At dawn, I tried to stop my thoughts by pulling the covers over my face, but images appeared anyway. I started seeing paintings of you. Some were realistic: one was of you when you were a girl sitting on a window bench, one was a portrait where your face was pale but your eyes were so green. What was strange was that I could see the details as if I had already painted them. I stayed all day in bed. The leg cast was heavy; I could not move, anyway. I had a bell that I used to call for Kata's assistance. Up the winding staircase she'd come, carrying a tray with a rattling cup of tea. Or I heard the patter of her footsteps going down the steps as she scurried around getting my box of watercolors and paper I'd left in the breakfast room.

Now two weeks later, I've started to move around. I sat on the terrace and made some sketches of the horses grazing. Their legs are a bit crooked and their backs swayed but I like them anyway as their expressions are kind. The next day it rained so I was stuck inside, and wandered around from room to room. The idea of painting you kept coming to mind, but I could not start. It was too soon, I said to myself as an excuse, but I think I'm scared of failing, of not being able to represent you in a knowable way. And what if I really could paint you and it did somehow make you more alive? And, if you ever could come alive again, would we know what to say to each other?

Yesterday I spent time in the stables, limping on the rubber heel of my walking cast. I brushed the horses as they munched their hay and took sips of water from the trough. This I can do, I thought. I wrapped my fingers around the smooth wood of the brush handle. The bristles made a clean path as I moved the brush down Pavo's neck while his eyes opened and closed, his long lashes rising and dipping.

Recently my dreams are about being broken. Thrown from a galloping horse. Falling from a ladder. I heard a bone crack in the last dream, and in it I could not move, could not wake up. When I finally did wake up, I was afraid to try to move, afraid the dream was endless. My memory is mysterious. I know it's mine, but I don't understand why it comes on its own. Why are those thoughts impossible to control? A feeling comes over me while painting; the sound of a door creaking open makes me look up, for you; blurry apparitions of you appear—and there you are, shimmering, then disappearing while floating away. Even with the photograph by my bed of you smiling, of you holding me, and with stories Zofie tells, I was too young to remember what you were like.

It is late afternoon. This morning I hobbled up the narrow stairs into Zofie's third-story office. She had just put the phone back onto its receiver and was gazing out over the view of the orchard. For a moment before she noticed me, I stood in the door and looked at her: at her thick auburn hair tied back with a ribbon, at her alert expression on her pretty face, at her hazel eyes which become especially bright when she's interested. I was about to begin to tell her that I might not have the nerve to ride again, that I was sure I was failing her as a daughter, but she looked up at me and said, "Nata, I'm so glad you came up here. We need a break. An excursion to town. The museum has an exhibit of landscape paintings. Let's check it out."

Zofie closed her engagement book, pushed back her chair, and said, "And guess what, that was the tourism office that called. We have bookings to stay in our house. There'll be a couple from Dresden, bikers from Hamburg, and, on the weekend after Easter, a family of three from Wales. Can you imagine? I've never even thought of people coming all the way to Bohemia from Wales."

Dede Reed is a writer and photographer who lives on the Eastern Shore in Maryland.

Made in the USA
Middletown, DE
24 November 2017